NIGHTMARE STAIRS

and

ROOM 13

Also available by Robert Swindells, and published by
Doubleday/Corgi Yearling Books:

ROBERT SWINDELLS

Nightmare Stairs

and

Room 13

Corgi Yearling Books

NIGHTMARE STAIRS and ROOM 13 2-in-1
A CORGI YEARLING BOOK 0440 866251

NIGHTMARE STAIRS
First published in Great Britain in 1997 by Doubleday
an imprint of Random House Children's Books
Corgi Yearling edition published 1998

ROOM 13
First published in Great Britain in 1989 by Doubleday
an imprint of Random House Children's Books
Corgi Yearling editions published 1990, 2000

This 2-in-1 Corgi Yearling edition published exclusively for Scholastic 2003

1 3 5 7 9 10 8 6 4 2

Papers used by Random House Children's Books are natural, recyclable products
made from wood grown in sustainable forests. The manufacturing processes
conform to the environmental regulations of the country of origin.

Corgi Yearling Books are published by Random House Children's Books,
61–63 Uxbridge Road, London W5 5SA,
a division of The Random House Group Ltd,
in Australia by Random House Australia (Pty) Ltd,
20 Alfred Street, Milsons Point, Sydney, NSW 2061, Australia,
in New Zealand by Random House New Zealand Ltd,
18 Poland Road, Glenfield, Auckland 10, New Zealand,
and in South Africa by Random House (Pty) Ltd,
Endulini, 5A Jubilee Road, Parktown 2193, South Africa

THE RANDOM HOUSE GROUP Limited Reg. No. 954009
www.kidsatrandomhouse.co.uk

A CIP catalogue record for this book is available from the British Library.

Printed and bound in Great Britain by Cox & Wyman Ltd, Reading, Berkshire

NIGHTMARE
STAIRS

For Art and Catfish

CHAPTER ONE

Here's a riddle:

> *No vampire, ghost nor bug-a-boo*
> *I live and breathe and play, like you*
> *Yet I was murdered long ago*
> *Now tell me – how can this be so?*

Not easy, right? True though – every word.
If you're not doing anything special I'll tell you
all about it but I have to warn you – it's weird.
Seriously weird.

Listen.

CHAPTER TWO

My first word was Mama. Well, whose isn't? It was my second word which caused a ripple, giving rise to one of those stories you find in every family. It goes like this.

I was fourteen months old, starting to toddle. Mum was dusting the room. She'd taken the framed photos off the sideboard and dumped them in an armchair. Family snaps. One was a black and white shot of Mum's parents in their garden. As Mum dusted the sideboard I was trying out my legs, lurching from one piece of furniture to another, and I arrived at this particular chair and picked up the photo. Mum saw me out of the corner of her eye and turned to take the thing away from me, afraid I might fall and smash the glass, and as she bent towards me I put my finger over my grandad's face and said, 'Bob.'

Not an earth-shattering event I admit, but it gave Mum a bit of a turn for two reasons. One, his name *had* been Bob, and two, both he and Grandma had died before I was born. I don't remember the incident myself, but apparently Mum gazed at me for a minute, dumbfounded, then shouted for Dad, and when Dad came I jabbed the same spot and said it again, quite distinctly. 'Bob.' Whereupon apparently they looked at me, then at each other, then burst out laughing. As I said, I remember nothing about it, but it seems they laughed so hard they had to hold each other up to keep from collapsing on the floor. They thought it was pure coincidence you see, because there was no way I could actually know the old guy's name. I was a baby, making baby noises, and twice I'd produced the same syllable which sounded remarkably like my late grandad's name.

And that's where they were wrong.

CHAPTER THREE

I had nightmares. I'd wake up screaming and Mum would come. The nightmares were always about falling but she didn't know that. How could she when I hadn't learned to talk? You've heard the expression 'nameless fear', I suppose? Well, that's what *my* fear was back then. Nameless. Mum'd hold me. Rock me. Murmur words I didn't understand but was comforted by, till I went back to sleep.

As I grew older I learned the words for what frightened me at night. 'Falling,' I'd sob when I was two or three, clinging to my mother's nightie. 'Frightened. Hurts.' I understood what she was saying to me by then of course. 'Not falling,' she'd say. 'Mummy's got you. It was a dream, darling. Just a silly old dream.' God, she must have had the patience of a saint. Remember, this had been happening three, four times a week ever since I was born and she was always there. Always gentle.

I think I was four the night she realized there might be something significant about my dream, the night I felt her body go stiff. I know I hadn't started school. I'd woken screaming as usual at some unearthly hour and she'd come and was holding me and I told her how I'd been standing at the top of some dark stairs and had fallen.

She went stiff and pushed me out at arm's length, looking into my eyes. 'Who's been talking to you, Kirsty?' she asked. Her voice sounded funny and I was scared. 'Who was it, darling?'

I didn't understand. I do now, but I was *four*, for goodness' sake. I thought I'd done something terrible. She was hurting me too – holding my arms really tightly. I burst into tears. If I'd known then what I know now I'd have understood what was bugging her, but I didn't. When I started crying she hugged me and rocked me, and she never went stiff like that again in all the years that followed but all the same it was different somehow. Her presence no longer consoled me quite as it had before. Presently I learned not to cry out on waking, and she and Dad thought my nightmare phase was at an end.

If only.

CHAPTER FOUR

I've laid these glimpses of my fascinating infancy on you without even introducing myself. Sorry. I'm Kirsty. Kirsty Miller. I'm thirteen. I've got a brother called Joe who's away at university. He's going to be a psychologist. I've no sisters. When I was little I used to wish for a sister but I'm not bothered now. There's a lot to be said for being the only kid at home.

Mum and Dad are teachers. Mum is Deputy Head at Cutler's Hill Primary, where I was till a couple of years ago. *That*'s no fun, by the way – being a teacher's kid. The others think you're getting special treatment and they're right, but not the way they mean. I swear Mum picked on me all the time just to show I wasn't getting favours. Dad is Head of English at Bessamer

Comp which is *not* where I am, thank God. I'm at Fettler's.

I've mentioned my Grandad Bob, who's dead. He smoked sixty fags a day and that killed him. Forty-nine. Six foot tall. Four and a half stone. You can see it happening in the photo. That stoop. Those haunted eyes and sunken cheeks. A man who knows his days are numbered.

His wife – my mum's mum – was called Elizabeth. She lived twenty-one years as a widow and died ten months before I was born. She lived in Nine Beeches, the poshest part of Yaxley. You can see the front of the cottage behind her and Grandad in the snapshot. I've seen it in real life as well, but I'll save that story till later.

My other grandparents – Dad's mum and dad – are alive and kicking. Kath and Steve, they're called. My grandad's got an unusual job. He used to work in the steel industry, same as most people in Yaxley, but that's gone. Now he's at the airport, supervising a team that cleans out planes. I'm not kidding. It's a hectic job. They've ten minutes to remove every scrap of litter, hoover down the aisles, dispose

14

of sick-bags, straighten magazines, take any unused meals from the galley and load it with fresh ones for the next flight. Ten minutes. The good thing about it is, he gets to keep the unused meals. You'd think they'd serve them on the next flight but they don't, so Steve and Kath practically live on airline food without ever leaving the ground.

And that's my family, except for my Auntie Anne. I haven't mentioned her yet because she's special. She deserves a page all to herself, and here it comes.

CHAPTER FIVE

She's Mum's big sister, Auntie Anne, but they're not a bit alike. Or if they are *I* can't see it. Mum's nice, you know? A really nice person – the sort who'll go out of her way to do someone a good turn, even a complete stranger. Auntie Anne isn't. No way. I'll tell you the sort of person *she* is. Suppose she's in the car park and it's Saturday afternoon and the place is full, right? She's loaded her shopping into the boot and she's ready to leave when she notices someone waiting for her space. Instead of starting up and pulling away like she meant to, she'll find a cloth and get out and start working her way round the car, really slowly, doing the windows and mirrors. They don't *need* doing – she's making the guy wait, that's all. And if he gives up and moves on she's really glad. I know she's my auntie but I've no time for her. In fact I hate her and I always have.

Here's another family story. When I was about two days old, Mum gave me to Auntie Anne to hold. I'd been fed, burped and changed and was sleepily content, but the second my auntie took hold of me I started screaming and kicking. I made such a racket, Mum was scared I might blow myself to fragments. She snatched me out of her sister's arms and five seconds later I was fast asleep.

I bet Auntie Anne wasn't bothered. She's hardly the maternal type. She's married, but she and Uncle Brian have no kids. Anyway, that story is just another piece in the jigsaw I started putting together last summer. It builds into a pretty weird picture, as you'll find out.

CHAPTER SIX

I was seven when we stopped to look at Grandma Elizabeth's old cottage. It was a Sunday in spring and we were out for a drive in the Volvo – Dad and Mum, Joe and me. I don't remember where we were going and it doesn't matter. Our route took us through Nine Beeches and Mum said something to Dad. He stopped the car and we got out.

'Oh look, Ken – they've *ruined* it,' groaned Mum as we peered over the gate at the house she'd grown up in. 'All those lovely old trees, gone. And look at that *hideous* dormer.' She pointed and I said, 'That's where the Glory Hole used to be.'

Mum glanced at me sharply. 'What?'

'The Glory Hole.' I could *see* it in my

mind's eye – a dim loft crammed with junk.

Mum squatted, her hands on my shoulders, gazing into my face. 'How do you know *that*, Kirsty? Who's talked to you about the cottage, darling?'

I shook my head. 'N-nobody's talked to me, Mum.'

'Oh, come on, Kirsty – somebody *must* have. How else would you know we called the loft the Glory Hole?'

Dad looked down at her. 'It could be any one of a number of people, Sylvia. Your sister. My parents. You might even have mentioned it yourself.'

She shook her head. 'I haven't, Ken. I *know* I haven't.'

'Well then, it must've been one of the others. It's not important, is it?'

'I – suppose not.' She straightened up and sighed. 'It's just . . . oh, I don't know. Can we leave, please? I wish we hadn't seen the place like this.'

We got back in the Volvo and drove on. Joe and I were fratching on the back seat and I suppose Mum thought I wouldn't hear when she murmured, 'There's something not quite right about that child, Ken.' She meant me of course, and I knew she was right. There *was* something not quite right about me, but five more years were to pass before I'd know what it was.

CHAPTER SEVEN

Something not quite right. When I was eight we were doing World War Two at school. Mum wasn't my teacher that year. We had a man, Mr Newell. He was telling us about bombing. The Blitz, as it was called. When enemy bombers were coming a siren used to sound to warn people so they could get in their shelters. Mr Newell had a cassette with the siren on it. He put it on, and as soon as I heard that siren something happened to me. Something scary.

It was like a video switched on in my head. I was in this big dim place – a great high room full of people and – I don't know – machinery I guess. The siren was drawing a wavy line in the air. Everybody was moving towards these big doors. Lights were going out. The doors opened and everybody spilled out into a sort of yard. It was dark and cold and you could tell from the shiny paving that it had just stopped raining. I was watching all this but I was *there* too. I can't explain. Anyway we had to cross this yard and go down some stone stairs. Behind the siren was a droning noise and now and then a loud, flat bang. A finger of light was moving across the sky. I'd nearly reached the stairs when there was a terrific flash and something slammed into me so hard that I flew sideways into some bins or boxes or something. I cried out. At once the video shut off and I was back in the classroom with everybody staring.

Mr Newell had stopped the cassette player and was frowning across at me. 'Are you all right, Kirsty Miller?'

'Y-yes, sir.'

'Oh good. For a minute there I thought the bombs had got you.'

Everybody laughed.

At breaktime Sally came up to me. Sally Armitage, my best friend at Cutler's Hill. 'That was *great*,' she giggled. 'The siren, and this bloodcurdling scream at the end of it. I don't know how you *dared*.'

I shrugged and smiled. It hadn't been a case of daring, but I couldn't explain that to Sally. Not when I couldn't explain it to *myself*.

CHAPTER EIGHT

I was still having the nightmares. Two, three times a week. Night*mare*, I should say, because it was always the same one. It went like this:

I'm in the dark at the top of the stairs. Steep, narrow stairs. I have to get myself down those stairs but there's something wrong with my legs. They're stiff. It hurts me to walk. I'm standing there, sort of gathering myself to make the effort when I see movement out of the corner of my eye. Somebody or some*thing* comes out of the spare bedroom, fast and quiet. I don't even have time to feel scared. Whoever or whatever it is puts a hand or paw in the middle of my back and shoves and I topple forward, crashing down the stairs in a chaos of terror, shock and pain.

I never hit the bottom. I wake up, damp and

shaking. For a short time I can actually feel the pain, hear the crashing row my falling body makes. I lie gasping, knowing that if I ever reach the foot of the stairs asleep, I'll never wake.

Sometimes in the evenings I'd overhear Mum and Dad talking. What kid doesn't? Mostly it was stuff I wasn't interested in. Money. Relatives. People at work. Stuff that happened years ago before I was born. Now and then though, I'd overhear something that'd ring a bell. A distant bell.

Like the night Mum got on to the war. We'd just watched an old film about London in the Blitz. I'd gone through to the kitchen to put the kettle on and I heard Mum say to Dad, 'They show the explosions and the fires and the falling buildings, but you never see what it *did* to people – how their lives were ruined. Take my mother – hit by the blast the night they bombed Viner's. Knocked her halfway across the yard. Smashed her legs. Fifteen, she was. Fifteen, and she never walked again without pain.'

Yeah, you've got it. My one-girl video show

two years back in old Newell's class. I'd forgotten all about it, but it came back with a
bang that night, I can tell you. My heart kicked
me in the ribs. I swallowed. Went cold. I made
the tea and when I carried it through Mum'd
switched channels, but I didn't enjoy the stuff
we gawped at after that. Couldn't concentrate.

CHAPTER NINE

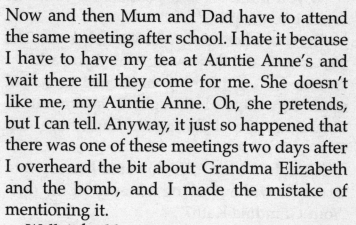

Now and then Mum and Dad have to attend the same meeting after school. I hate it because I have to have my tea at Auntie Anne's and wait there till they come for me. She doesn't like me, my Auntie Anne. Oh, she pretends, but I can tell. Anyway, it just so happened that there was one of these meetings two days after I overheard the bit about Grandma Elizabeth and the bomb, and I made the mistake of mentioning it.

Well, it had been preying on my mind. Was it just coincidence, that strange experience I'd had when I was eight, or was it possible I'd seen a bit out of Grandma Elizabeth's life? I'd spent two nights lying awake thinking about it. In fact it was doing my head in. I felt I had to share it with somebody or go crazy. So when tea was over and Uncle Brian left the table and went upstairs I took a deep breath and plunged in.

'Auntie Anne?'

'Yes?' She looked at me over the rim of her cup. She had these very thin, plucked eyebrows and lots of green and purple eyeliner. Made her look like Queen Whatsit. Nefertiti.

'D'you think . . . is it possible for someone to see into the past?'

She shook her head. 'No, Kirsty, it is not. The past is over and done with. Why d'you ask?'

'Oh, I . . . something happened at school once. Ages ago. I thought I saw a bit of Grandma's life.' I shrugged. 'Can't have, can I?'

'Grandma's life?' She lowered her cup into its saucer without taking her eyes off my face. 'Your Grandma Kath?'

I shook my head. 'Grandma Elizabeth.'

She sniffed. 'You never *knew* Grandma Elizabeth, Kirsty. How could you possibly see any part of *her* life?'

I pulled a face. 'I dunno. It's daft. We were doing about the war. The teacher had this tape.' I told her what had happened when the siren went. She listened, her bottom lip caught between her teeth. I noticed that some of her lipstick had got onto her two front teeth. When I'd finished she said, 'Imagination, Kirsty, that's all it was. The lesson caught your imagination and you felt as if you were *there*, just for a minute.'

I nodded. 'Yes, but then a couple of nights ago we watched this film about the war, and Mum mentioned something that happened to Grandma Elizabeth and it was the *same*. Exactly the same. My legs. *Her* legs, I mean.'

She got up then, so suddenly it made me jump. Her face looked white, though that might have been my imagination too. 'Nonsense,' she rapped. 'Nobody sees the past. It's gone, dear. Dead and gone.'

She didn't mean the *dear* bit, I can tell you. She turned her back and started crashing dishes in the sink and it was obvious I'd upset her. After a minute I got up and grabbed a tea towel and she said, 'Leave them to drain, please.' Snapped at me, you know? So I rehung the flipping tea towel and stalked off into her immaculate front room to watch the telly. Neither of us mentioned the matter when Mum and Dad came for me but they *must've* felt the atmosphere. So. Telling someone hadn't helped a bit, and I hated going to my auntie's even more after that.

Chapter Ten

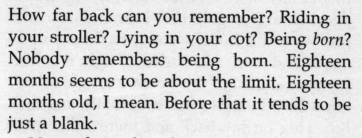

How far back can you remember? Riding in your stroller? Lying in your cot? Being *born*? Nobody remembers being born. Eighteen months seems to be about the limit. Eighteen months old, I mean. Before that it tends to be just a blank.

Not with me though. I can remember being – what – a few minutes old? An hour or two? I *think* I can anyway.

You know the nightmare I told you about? Standing at the top of the stairs and being shoved and falling? And I said I always wake up before I hit the bottom? Well, that's not quite true. Not quite. Sometimes – just now and then – I stay asleep a bit longer and the dream goes on, and that's where it gets really scary. I don't even want to talk about it but I've got to because that's where the last piece is. The last piece of the jigsaw, I mean.

What happens is this. I'm falling. Everything's whirling, crashing, pain. Then suddenly it's still and quiet and there's this – fading away. Everything's fading away. The fear. The light. The pain. I'm sinking into warm soft darkness where things don't matter any more and it's really, really restful and I want it to go on for ever and ever, and just when I think it's going to there's noise again, and pain, and flashes of light that hurt my eyes and all of this goes on for oh, I don't know how long. It stops eventually, and then I'm lying on my back and there's this great fuzzy brightness and it's really cold and there's something rough against my skin and everything – hurts. There's movement – things moving, but I can't see properly. Everything's fuzzy. I think, *Is this Heaven? Hell?* I'm scared. I don't seem to be able to move much. Can't get up. I reach out my hand and it finds something. A warm thing, but hard. I curl my fingers round it. Hold on to it. Something moves in front of the light. It swoops, becoming a face. A face I don't know, smiling into mine and that's when I realize I'm a baby. *That* wakes me up, I can tell you.

And then they wonder why newborn babies howl.

CHAPTER ELEVEN

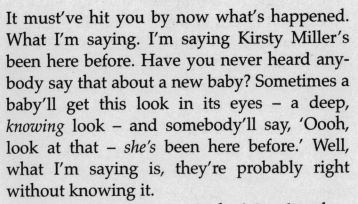

It must've hit you by now what's happened. What I'm saying. I'm saying Kirsty Miller's been here before. Have you never heard anybody say that about a new baby? Sometimes a baby'll get this look in its eyes – a deep, *knowing* look – and somebody'll say, 'Oooh, look at that – *she's* been here before.' Well, what I'm saying is, they're probably right without knowing it.

Oh yes, I know it's far-fetched. I realize that. It was months before *I* could get my head round it but, you see, the evidence was all there. I knew the layout of the cottage at Nine Beeches, though I'd never been inside. I knew its loft used to be known as the Glory Hole. I knew Grandad Rodwell's first name – Bob – though nobody had ever used the name in my hearing. And I knew exactly what had happened to Grandma Elizabeth the night they bombed Viner's – I'd seen it, *felt* it, without ever leaving my seat in Mr Newell's class at Cutler's Hill Primary. And I was pretty sure I knew something else as well – something terrible, which nobody knew but me and a certain other person.

I struggled with all this stuff for months. Wrestled it in bed at night. I was desperate to tell someone but I didn't dare. Especially not the last bit – the awful suspicion I harboured about a member of my family. I was afraid that if I told anyone they'd think I was crazy and have me committed to one of those psychiatric hospitals they never let you out of. And I actually *felt* crazy. I wasn't sleeping. Couldn't concentrate at school. It felt like my life was crumbling. Falling apart. I had to *do* something.

One Saturday last autumn – it was the start of the October break – I was helping Mum with the vegetables. Dad was outside doing something to the car. I was at breaking point – really tensed up, and I said, 'Mum – how did Grandma Elizabeth die?' They'd never talked about it, see? Not in my hearing. All I knew was that she'd died a few months before I was born.

Mum gave me a funny look. 'What made you think about *that* all of a sudden, darling?' All of a sudden. That's a laugh for a start. I pulled a face. 'I think I know anyway, Mum. She fell downstairs, didn't she?'

'Who told you that, Kirsty?'

'Nobody. It happened at the cottage, didn't it? At Nine Beeches?'

'*Somebody* must have told you, or you wouldn't know. *I* certainly never mentioned it. Was it Auntie Anne?'

I shook my head. 'I *told* you, Mum – it was nobody. I just – know, that's all. Why is it such a secret anyway? A lot of old people die falling downstairs.'

Mum nodded. 'I know, darling, but you see – there was your nightmare. Do you remember your nightmare? About falling? You used to get it almost every night. Your dad and I thought if you knew your grandma died from a fall it might make your nightmare worse. Sounds silly now but we did, and that's why we never mentioned it.'

I shook my head. 'I doubt if it'd have made

any difference to my nightmare, Mum. Anyway you can tell me now, 'cause I know already.'

She shrugged. 'There's really nothing to tell, darling. Your grandma's legs were bad because of the war. She shouldn't have stayed on at the cottage after your grandad died but she wouldn't give it up. The staircase was steep and dark. One day she must have slipped or tripped or something, at the top. The postman found her next morning. He had a package for her, and when she didn't answer his knock he looked through the slot and there she was at the foot of the stairs. Her neck was broken. The doctor said she would have died instantly.'

She didn't, I thought. Not quite. There was no pain, but she felt everything going away.

'Poor Grandma,' I murmured, scraping diced carrots into the pan with the back of the knife. 'Dying alone like that.'

Alone my foot, I thought, lighting the gas. It was amazing how angry I felt.

CHAPTER TWELVE

Who was my anger directed at? Go on – have a guess. If you think it was directed at Auntie Anne, you're absolutely right. Well done.

I've told you a bit about my auntie. She's the one who'll hang on to a parking space for the pleasure of screwing up a total stranger. She's also the one in my dream who comes out of the spare bedroom and shoves me off the top step.

Oh yes. Of course I didn't realize till last summer. Or maybe I'd known all along but wouldn't let myself believe it. Because it is sort of unbelievable, isn't it? Her own *mother*, for goodness' sake.

In case you think I was jumping to conclusions – branding Auntie Anne a murderer on the strength of a dream and a coincidence –

I'd better tell you something I forgot before. Remember I said we stopped once when I was seven to look at Grandma's old cottage? And Joe and I were fratching on the back seat while Mum and Dad chuntered on, and I heard Mum say, *There's something not quite right about that child.* Remember? Right. Well, Dad said something too. About the cottage. I didn't get it at the time, but I do now. By golly I do. This is what he said: *It's a pity your mother didn't get around to changing her will. If she had, we'd be living in the cottage and that ugly dormer would never have been built.*

Well. Doesn't take a university education, does it? To sort that one out, I mean. Those words of Dad's came back to me when Mum said Grandma ought not to have stayed on at the cottage. I didn't say anything. Not straight away. I went up to my room and had a think, and then I asked Mum another question, and her answer completed the jigsaw.

'Mum?' We'd eaten the meal. Mum and I were doing the dishes. Dad was in the front room, watching sport.

'Yes, dear?'

'What did Dad mean when he said it's a

pity Grandma Elizabeth didn't change her will?'

She frowned. 'When did he say that, Kirsty? *I* don't remember.'

'Oh, it was years ago. In the car. What did he mean?'

Mum sighed. 'Well, I really don't understand why you're interested, dear, but if you must know it was like this. Your grandma's will left the cottage to Auntie Anne as the elder daughter, but when Grandma learned that Anne and Brian didn't intend having children, she decided to change her will so that I would get it. We had Joe, you see, and were trying for a girl. Unfortunately she didn't get around to it straightaway, and then she had her accident and that was that.'

Makes you think, doesn't it? Made *me* think.

Chapter Thirteen

As I've said, it was October break. I'd just finished my first half-term at Fettler's, which hadn't been easy with all this stuff building up inside my head. Anyway, it meant I had a week, and I decided to spend it looking for evidence of Auntie Anne's guilt.

I'd no idea how to begin. I wondered what would happen if I simply confronted her. *I know your secret, Auntie Anne. You murdered your mother to get the cottage, didn't you?* Would she break down? Confess? Great if she did, but what if she didn't? What if she got blazingly angry, ordered me out of her house and called Dad? *Kirsty's flipped her lid.* And what if I'm wrong after all and she's completely innocent?

No, I couldn't proceed that way. I couldn't

41

confide in anybody either. I spent most of Sunday sitting on a bench in Yaxley town centre, thinking. Everything was shut so I had the place practically to myself. At three o'clock it started to drizzle and I moved into C&A's doorway. There was this dummy in the window – a guy in a dark suit with a briefcase, reading the *Financial Times*, and that's what gave me the idea. It'd be in the paper, wouldn't it, when my grandma was found dead? Not the *Financial Times* of course, but the *Yaxley Star*. It was full of stuff like that. I could go to the public library and look through back numbers of the paper. I knew roughly when it happened. Ten months before I was born. I was born in April 1984, so Grandma Elizabeth must've died sometime in June 1983. So, all I had to do was look through every edition of the *Star* for that month and I'd find it. Of course it might not tell me anything I didn't already know but on the other hand it might, and anyway I had to start somewhere.

I couldn't do it that day because the library doesn't open Sundays. I walked home through the rain feeling better than I had for months.

Not terrific, you know, but better. At least now I was *doing* something instead of just brooding, but if I'd known what I was letting myself in for, I think I might have left it alone.

CHAPTER FOURTEEN

A funny thought came into my head in bed that night. Funny peculiar, not funny ha-ha. Here it is. Grandma Elizabeth was Mum's mother, so if I was her reincarnation *I* was Mum's mother too, in a way. I was hers and she was mine. Wonder what she'd say if I told her?

Needless to say, I didn't. Next morning I walked into town and went to the library. I'd pictured myself sitting with a stack of fusty old papers, turning hundreds and hundreds of yellow-edged pages and sneezing from the dust, but it wasn't like that at all. Instead I found myself sitting in front of a contraption with a screen, a bit like a computer monitor. All the papers have been photographed in miniature on like film. All you have to do is feed the film through the machine and pages come up on screen. Microfiche, it's called. You operate it by hand so you can go as fast or as slow as you want. Once you know how to do it it's dead easy, and far better than searching through actual papers.

So there I sat, feeding and reading. I got distracted a few times, like there was this piece about a spacecraft, *Pioneer 10*, which had become the first man-made object to travel beyond the solar system. I stopped and read it because I'm into stuff like that, but I found what I was looking for too.

June 14th 1983. That's when the postman found her, so she probably died on the 13th, which struck me as appropriate. It was a short piece – ten or twelve lines. I'd brought a notebook and I copied the item into it, word for word. I could probably have asked for a photocopy or something, but I didn't want people knowing what I was doing. Here's what it said:

WIDOW FOUND DEAD

An elderly woman was found dead at her home in Nine Beeches today after apparently falling downstairs. Mrs Elizabeth Rodwell, a widow, lived alone. Her body was discovered by postman Mr Derek Lassiter, who peered through the letter slot after Mrs Rodwell failed to answer his knock. Mr Lassiter contacted the police but a spokesman told our reporter, 'There'll be an inquest, but as far as we are concerned this was a domestic tragedy. There is no question of foul play.'

Mrs Rodwell was the mother of Mrs Anne Tasker, well known locally as manager of Whiteleys estate agency. She also leaves a second daughter, and one grandchild.

That was it. The only surprise was that bit about Auntie Anne and Whiteleys. The place is still there but my aunt has no connection with it, and it was news to me she ever did. I underlined it in my notebook and scrolled through nine more copies of the *Star* till I located a report of the inquest. Death by misadventure,

46

the coroner had decided. I jotted it down, wondering if this was the only time the guy'd been wrong. Then I left the library. I felt like Sherlock flipping Holmes, except he'd probably have known what to do next and I didn't.

CHAPTER FIFTEEN

I went to Island in the shopping mall. It's a coffee bar. I got a Coke and sat at a corner table, thinking.

What am I trying to do? Easy – prove that my Auntie Anne pushed her mother downstairs. All right – what proof do I have so far? Answer – none at all. There's my dream of course, but I doubt whether that would impress the police. Can't you just see it?

Sergeant, you've got to arrest my auntie.

Oh, and why's that, Miss?

She murdered my grandma.

Did she now? How d'you know?

I dreamed it. And anyway I was my grandma. In a previous life.

Non-starter, right? So. I need *proof.* Something solid. What I really need to find out is what Auntie Anne was doing on June 13th 1983 – the day Grandma fell downstairs. Trouble is, it was fourteen years ago. Who's going to remember? *She* will, but I can hardly ask her, can I? Uncle Brian might, but I can't ask him either.

All right – what do I know already? Well, I know it was a Monday because the story was in Tuesday's *Star*. So it was a working day. And I know Anne was managing Whiteleys, so presumably she was there. Was anybody there *with* her? And if someone was, is that person still working at Whiteleys now? Doubt it. Fourteen years ago. But it's a start, isn't it? Something to do. Go along to Whiteleys and ask. Make enquiries, like a private detective.

They were having a slow day at Whiteleys. No customers. There was just this guy behind the counter. Plumpish, thirty-something, ginger moustache, and a woman in a glass cubicle behind with a VDU. 'Yes?' goes the guy as I walk through the door. No enthusiasm – I'm too young to be looking for a house.

'I – wonder if you can help me?'

He smiles faintly. 'Depends. School project, is it?'

'No. I'm looking for someone.'

'We do homes, petal, not missing persons.' Ignorant pig.

'It's someone who might have worked here with my auntie, fourteen years ago.'

'Fourteen *years*?' He shakes his head. 'Fourteen years ago I was living in Exeter, darling. How would *I* know about somebody who worked here then?'

I glance past his shoulder. 'Perhaps that lady . . . ?'

'No chance. She's been here three weeks.'

'Oh. Well . . . do you keep records – you know . . . ?'

'No records, sweetheart. Just houses. Look.' He spreads his pudgy palms on the counter and leans towards me. 'You're wasting your time, which probably doesn't matter, and mine, which does. Why don't you go away and come back when you're looking for somewhere to live, *then* we might be able to help you.'

I'm the quiet type, you know? Hate making any kind of fuss, but this guy is so obnoxious –

so *slimy* – that I gaze into his piggy little eyes and say, 'You must be joking. I'd live in a rubbish skip before I'd come to a plonker like you.' I flounce out before his tiny brain can think up a reply.

CHAPTER SIXTEEN

Mum might know if anybody worked with Anne. They're sisters after all, but how can I ask her? She doesn't even know I know about my auntie's job at Whiteleys. If she finds out I'm prying into Anne's life she's going to want to know why, and I couldn't possibly explain.

What about Anne herself? Might it be possible to raise the subject of her past life casually, in the course of conversation? It wouldn't be easy. Auntie Anne and I don't *have* conversations. I don't even go near her house except when Mum and Dad have meetings, but I couldn't think of any other way, so I decided to give it a go.

What I did was, I pretended to be worried about my future. In actual fact I didn't give a hoot about my future, but Auntie Anne wasn't to know that. I sat in her neat shiny lounge and gave her some bull about the careers teacher at school asking us all what we wanted to be and me being the only girl who didn't know. I said I'd tried talking to Mum about it, but she'd said it was too soon to start worrying – I was only thirteen, for goodness' sake. Anne said, 'Your mother's right, Kirsty. It is too soon. You should be enjoying yourself while you can.'

I nodded. 'I know, but . . .' I looked at her. 'Have *you* ever had a job, Auntie Anne?' Dead innocent.

She nodded. 'Oh yes. More than one.'

'What were they?'

'Well – when I was sixteen I worked at a hairdresser's as a trainee. It didn't suit me so I moved to a fashion shop. I started as junior sales and rose to manageress at nineteen. I stayed there till I was twenty-two, then Whiteleys the estate agents opened their branch in Yaxley and advertised for a manager.' She smiled. 'They wanted a man really but I applied and was interviewed, and they must have been impressed because I got the job.' She smirked. 'Good salary, commission, company car. Not bad for a woman of twenty-two.' She's dead modest, my auntie. I hate her. I felt like saying, *Hmmm – a manager at twenty-two, then a murderer. Quite a career.* That'd have shut her up.

'Wow!' I pulled a face. 'I bet it was hard though. Did you have people under you? You know – staff?'

She smiled wryly. 'Staff'd be a bit of an exaggeration, Kirsty. I had Molly. Oh, and a woman who cleaned the place three evenings a week.'

'What did Molly do?'

My auntie shrugged. 'Secretarial work. Typing. Filing. Keeping the appointments book, answering the phone.'

'Is that a good job?'

Anne shook her head. 'No, not really. You want to set your sights a bit higher than Molly Barraclough, Kirsty.'

'Yes but *what*, Auntie Anne? Every job the teacher mentions sounds really boring. I want to do something interesting or exciting. D'you think travel agency work . . . ?'

It went on like that for a while, but I'd got

what I came for. The hardest bit was remembering the name while Auntie Anne went banging on. The minute I got outside I wrote it in my notebook.

Molly Barraclough.

CHAPTER SEVENTEEN

Tuesday morning. Dad had dashed off to some meeting. Mum and I were dossing over the breakfast table in our dressing gowns, sipping coffee. Mum was reading a letter from someone she was at college with.

'Mum?'

'Uh-huh?' She didn't look up.

'Who's Molly Barraclough?'

'Huh? I'm sorry, darling, *who* did you say?'

'Molly Barraclough.'

Now she glanced up. 'Where on earth did you hear Molly's name, Kirsty? I haven't seen Molly for . . . oh, must be ten years. Longer, probably.'

'Auntie Anne mentioned her once,' I lied truthfully.

'Hmm,' grunted Mum. 'Did she blush?'

'How d'you mean?'

Mum folded her letter and put it down. 'Molly worked for your auntie when she was manager at Whiteleys. Did you know Auntie Anne used to be a manager, darling?'

'Uh . . . I think she told me.'

'I bet she didn't tell you that when poor Molly started with multiple sclerosis she sacked her out of hand.' Mum pulled a face. 'Makes you a bit clumsy, MS. You drop things, knock things over.'

'So Auntie Anne sacked her?'

Mum nodded. 'Yes. She was a sweetie too. Always cheerful. I used to run into her sometimes in town after she left Whiteleys. She was living on the Flower Estate then but perhaps she moved away, or died.' She sighed. 'That's how it is, Kirsty – we come and we go. More coffee?'

Slow stuff, detective work. I helped with the dishes, then went to my room and wrote 'Flower Estate' in my notebook, next to Molly's name. It's called the Flower Estate because all the roads are named after wild flowers. It's a big sprawling place on a hillside. I was praying Mum was wrong – that

Molly Barraclough hadn't gone away.

I waited till I heard Mum start hoovering the front room, then slipped downstairs and got the phone book. I sat on my bed and looked up Barraclough. Turned out there were hundreds of Barracloughs in Yaxley – nearly two pages. I went straight to the initial M. There were seventeen M. Barracloughs, but I struck lucky because only three of them lived in Cattercliff, the district that includes the Flower Estate, and one of *them* wasn't on the estate itself.

So, two possibilities. I copied the numbers and addresses into my notebook. M. Barraclough of 22 Celandine Nook, and M. Barraclough of 34 Ragwort Drive. No way of knowing which was Molly. Neither, probably. Anyway, I'd call and ask for Molly. What I'd do if I got her I'd no idea.

CHAPTER EIGHTEEN

I didn't phone from home. Too risky. I went down town, to the library. They've got a row of public phones.

I called Celandine Nook. A woman picked up. 'Oh hello,' I said. 'Is this Molly Barraclough?'

'You must have the wrong number. There's no Molly here.' She hung up before I could apologize.

A woman answered at Ragwort Drive too. 'Oh hello,' I chirped. 'Am I speaking to Molly Barraclough?'

'Ye-es. Who is this?'

My heart kicked. I swallowed. 'Were you . . . did you once work at Whiteleys on Steeler Street?'

'That's right. Who's speaking please?'

'You don't know me, Ms Barraclough, but Anne Tasker is my auntie.'

'Anne . . . ? Oh, yes. Anne. So how can I help you, love?'

'I wondered if I could have a word with you.'

'What about?'

'About my auntie. Something that happened.'

'I'm sorry, I don't understand. Something that happened?'

'Well . . . something that *might* have happened, fourteen years ago. Something serious.'

'I still don't understand, dear. What's your name, by the way?'

'Oh, sorry. It's Kirsty. Kirsty Miller.'

'How old are you, Kirsty?'

'Thirteen. Look – it's *really* important, honestly. Couldn't we meet somewhere? In town?

'I – don't get out much these days. Trouble walking.'

'Oh, I'm sorry. Would it be OK if I came to see you? I know where you are.'

'Well . . . I suppose so, but I have to say

60

I'm mystified. When were you thinking of coming?'

'Oh, whenever's best for you, Ms Barraclough. No school this week.'

'Well – how would two o'clock this afternoon suit you?'

'That'd be fantastic.'

She chuckled. 'I can't promise it'll be fantastic, love, but there *is* a packet of chocolate biscuits somewhere if I can find it. Two o'clock, then?'

'On the dot. And thanks a lot.'

'A poet too, eh?' She chuckled again and hung up. I looked at my watch. Ten past ten. What could I usefully do for three hours or so? Sherlock Holmes would've done some opium and played his violin. I settled for coffee and piped music at Island.

CHAPTER NINETEEN

I bussed it out to the Flower Estate and found Ragwort Drive. Number 34 could have done with a paint job and the garden sorting. I took a deep breath, marched up the weedy path and knocked.

It took her ages to answer. When the door finally opened I found myself looking at a plumpish woman of about forty in a purple sweater and black leggings. She had a mop of frizzy grey hair and was propped on a single elbow-crutch. She smiled. 'Kirsty?'

'Y-yes. I'm sorry to . . .'

'It's all right, love. Come on in.' She swivelled a half turn on the crutch, making room. 'Through there. Sit yourself down. I'll be with you in a minute.' She shut the door and moved off along the hallway. I entered the living room, where a pair of two-seater settees took up most of the space. There was a low table with a TV and video, a gas fire, a glass and steel coffee table with a stack of newspapers and magazines at one end, a small bookcase, and in a corner a weeping fig in a square white tub. The blue carpet was faded and threadbare, especially round the doorway. I sat down on one of the settees and looked at a print of Salisbury Cathedral on the wall.

She came in, balancing a loaded tray in one trembling hand. I jumped up and took it, going, 'You should've . . . I would've . . .'

''S OK, love, thanks. Put it on the coffee table. That's right. Now.' She lowered herself into the other settee, laid the crutch along the floor and smiled. 'We'll have a nice cuppa, and you can tell me what this is about.'

Back at Island, I'd thought about how I might handle this. I'd decided it'd be best not to mention dreams and trances and stuff if I could help it, and certainly not reincarnation. I didn't want this woman thinking she'd let some sort of nutcase into her home. I wondered if I should offer to pour the tea, but disabled people can be sensitive about – you know – people thinking they can't do stuff, so in the end I left her to it. We sat, sipping tea and nibbling chocolate biscuits, and I said, 'I'm interested in the thirteenth and fourteenth of June 1983.'

Molly gave me a look. Half-smiling, half-quizzical. 'Are you now? As precise as that. Why?'

'Because that's when my grandma died.'

'Your grandma?'

I nodded. 'Elizabeth Rodwell, Ms Barraclough. Anne's mother.'

'Ah. Ah, yes.' She became still. Her eyes had a distant look and I knew she was somewhere else. In her cubicle at Whiteleys, perhaps. I waited, gazing at her. After a minute she came back, murmuring, 'I remember. Of course I do. How strange, after all this time.' She looked at me. 'She fell downstairs, didn't she? Your grandma, I mean.'

I nodded. My heart was racing. I hoped she couldn't tell. 'That's what I was told. It was before I was born, you see. Ten months before.'

'Yes.' She was holding her cup with the fingertips of both hands, gazing into it like someone reading the leaves. 'Why have you come to me? Why me? Surely your family . . . your mother . . .' She looked straight at me. 'What exactly are you looking for, Kirsty?'

I swallowed. What could I say? I shrugged. 'I . . . I'm not sure, Ms Barraclough. I . . .'

'Molly,' she corrected. 'Call me Molly.' She fixed me with her level gaze. 'You think . . . you suspect there was something unusual about your grandmother's death, don't you?' Her voice was soft, almost a whisper. I didn't say anything. I couldn't. All my life I'd been the only one. The sole custodian of a truly dreadful suspicion. Or that's what I'd always assumed. Now it seemed I might have been mistaken. Now there was Molly and suddenly it was out in the open, lying like some repulsive object in the silence between us. I tore my eyes from hers and stared at the carpet, my lower lip caught between my teeth. I could feel her looking at me. Looking at me.

I nodded.

CHAPTER TWENTY

'Ah.' She sipped some tea, watching me over the rim of the cup. I gazed into mine, thinking, if I don't say anything else – if I get up now and leave – it needn't go any further. It'll be a suspicion shared by two people, that's all. There'll be no need to *do* anything. But if I speak, my words will make it real, and then . . .

'What do you think happened, Kirsty?' She spoke softly. I felt her eyes on me. I looked at her.

'I think . . . I believe my aunt pushed my grandma, Molly.' There. It was out. Events would follow now. Consequences. It was inevitable.

Molly nodded. 'I believe so too, Kirsty. Always have. It was all too – convenient, you see. The way it worked out, I mean.'

'Convenient?'

She nodded. 'Yes. I think that's the right word.' She leaned forward, put her cup and saucer on the table and settled back, her right arm along the padded arm of the chair, her left in her lap. 'I might as well start at the beginning and tell you exactly what happened on those two days in 1983.' She sighed. 'I can't tell you how hard I've tried to forget about all of this over the years, Kirsty. It's haunted me, and perhaps this is why. Perhaps you were always meant to seek me out, with your big blue eyes and your disturbing questions.' She shrugged. 'Well anyway, this is how it was.

'One day in early June of 1983, a man came into the office. His name was Mr Abubaka Tefawa Shah.' Molly smiled. 'That name – Abubaka Tefawa Shah – is one of the reasons I've not been able to forget the incident in spite of my best endeavours. It's memorable. Sticks in the mind. And it wasn't just the name. He was a striking figure, Kirsty. Not the sort of man you normally come across in Yaxley. You could tell he was rich by the way he carried himself. His haircut. The way he spoke. And his clothes. The best, Kirsty. The very best.

Clothes like his place their wearer, just as this crummy sweater places me. Anyway, Mr Shah was anxious to acquire a property in Nine Beeches. It *must* be Nine Beeches – he wasn't interested in any other location.' She smiled. 'And as luck would have it, we hadn't anything in Nine Beeches at the time. Not a thing.

'Your aunt was distraught. Well – she could see as well as I could that Mr Shah would pay any price for what he wanted. It was a case of money no object, and your aunt was more than usually fond of money, Kirsty, if you'll forgive my saying so. She was desperate not to let this walking gold mine walk away, so she told him we were expecting something to come vacant any day. Leave your card, she said, and we'll call you as soon as things start moving. So he gave her a card and went off. I was sure we'd seen the last of him, because we weren't expecting anything in Nine Beeches at all. She'd lied to him about that, or I thought she had, but then—' Molly broke off, groping for the elbow-crutch. 'Look – I'm parched. Why don't I brew a fresh pot? You must be fed up of listening to me anyway.'

'No no, I'm not, but if you're parched, *I'll* make tea—'

'No you won't.' She hauled herself erect and leaned on the stick. 'You can bring the tray though, if you want to help.'

I didn't want to help. I didn't want tea. I wanted to hear the rest of the story, though I imagined I could guess most of it. Anyway, Molly was stumping towards the door so I picked up the tray and followed her.

CHAPTER TWENTY-ONE

When we'd settled ourselves with steaming cups and the last of the biscuits, Molly said, 'Now – where was I?'

'Mr Shah,' I prompted. 'He'd left his card.'

'Ah, yes. Well, a few days went by – about a week, I suppose – and then one afternoon your aunt stuck her head round my door and said she was popping out for a while. It wasn't unusual – she often did bits of shopping in office hours or had her hair done, so I didn't think anything of it. But when she came back a couple of hours later she told me to call Mr Shah and ask him to pop into the office when he'd got a minute, because she'd found a property at Nine Beeches he might be interested in. Now, there wasn't anything particularly strange about that, except there was nothing in the appointments book.' Molly broke off, sipped some tea and explained. 'You see, what normally happened was, somebody wanting to sell their house would phone Whiteleys and arrange for your aunt to go and view the property, explain our terms and so forth, and I'd write the appointment in the book. Well, I couldn't remember writing anything about Nine Beeches, and I *would* have remembered because of Mr Shah. So later, after I'd called him, I checked, and there was nothing. I was a bit puzzled, but I told myself Anne must have taken a call while I was at lunch or something and fixed the appointment herself, without writing it down. That would have been unusual but it had happened from time to time so I put it out of my mind, until next morning when she rang me at nine to say she'd be late, her mother had been found dead.'

Molly stopped and I murmured, 'Her mother was found on the fourteenth, but Anne knew about the cottage on the thirteenth – is *that* what you're saying?'

Molly nodded. I stared at the carpet for a few seconds, then looked at her. 'Why . . . why didn't you say something at the time, Molly? Mention it to somebody – the police? Surely there'd have been clues. Evidence.'

She shook her head. 'The postman called the police. It was they who broke in, found that your grandma was dead. If there'd been anything suspicious they'd have spotted it, but no.' She smiled tightly. 'Your aunt committed the perfect murder, Kirsty. That's what I've always believed, anyway.'

I nodded. Neither of us spoke for a while. I don't know what Molly was thinking, but I was wondering what I ought to do next. I mean, there'd be no proof now, would there? Not after fourteen years, but you can't just *leave* something like that, can you? You can't carry on with your life, knowing murder was committed. Having tea at the murderer's house, chatting with her about this and that. Especially when you were the victim in a previous life.

Molly broke the silence, clearing her throat. 'And you, Kirsty. What was it made you suspect your aunt?'

Ah well, I thought. It had to come. The six million dollar question. Now she finds out I'm bonkers. I pulled a face. 'I have this dream. This nightmare. Somebody shoves me downstairs. I've had it since I was a baby.'

Molly smiled, a Mona Lisa smile. I'd expected her to flip. Yell at me. Chuck me out of her house, but instead she smiled, like smiling at a secret thought, and she nodded. 'You're a dreamer too,' she murmured. 'I thought so.' Her smile broadened. 'Takes one to know one, as they say.'

I stared at her. 'You mean, you . . . ?'

'Oh, yes. I dream. Always have.' She spread her arms and looked down at herself. 'I even knew I was going to wind up like this, only I blocked it out. Didn't want to know. So you see, I know exactly how you feel.'

I didn't know what to say, my head was in such a whirl. 'That's great,' I stammered. 'I mean, not that you're . . . you know, but to know I'm not the only one. I thought I was going crazy—' I broke off, then ploughed on. Might as well get it over. Drag it into the open, see what happens. I pulled a face. 'Trouble is, there's more, Molly. Not just the dreaming,

73

and if I tell you everything you *will* think I'm loopy. I know you will.'

Molly shook her head. 'I doubt it, Kirsty. Try me.'

So I did.

CHAPTER TWENTY-TWO

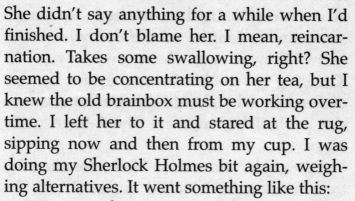

She didn't say anything for a while when I'd finished. I don't blame her. I mean, reincarnation. Takes some swallowing, right? She seemed to be concentrating on her tea, but I knew the old brainbox must be working overtime. I left her to it and stared at the rug, sipping now and then from my cup. I was doing my Sherlock Holmes bit again, weighing alternatives. It went something like this:

You can't choose to do nothing. Not now. So, you've got to prove that Auntie Anne murdered her mother.

There are two ways of bringing a criminal to justice. You either produce strong evidence – fingerprints, fibres – something that places the suspect at the scene of the crime – or you get a confession. You're not going to find fingerprints or fibres or anything else at the cottage after all this time, even if you could get in there to search, which you can't. The only other thing would be if Auntie Anne had written something down about the murder – in a diary, say – but Auntie Anne's not that thick. If she *did* commit anything to paper at the time, which is highly unlikely, she'd have destroyed it years ago. So. It'll have to be a confession. But how the heck do you get someone to confess to murder when they know they've got clean away with it? Knowing it'd get her banged up for the rest of her life, why should Auntie Anne admit she pushed her mother? She'd have to be crazy.

'Incredible,' murmured Molly, derailing my train of thought. I looked quizzical and she smiled. 'You may not believe this, Kirsty, but I've lived before too. In the 1920s. I was a boy. A little boy. I drowned, playing near a dam. Fell in and drowned. Nine years old.'

I gazed at her, this person like me, and she was right. I couldn't believe it. It seemed too good to be true.

'How . . . how d'you know you were nine,

76

Molly, and that it was the Twenties? Where . . .
I mean, I don't get *detail* like that.'

She nodded. 'I know what you mean, love.
I don't dream that clearly either. What
happened was, I was out walking – this was
before my . . . you know? Anyway I was in a
spot I'd never visited before and I came round
a corner and bang – I *knew* the place. There was
a row of cottages and I thought, *That's where
Raymond lived*. Last house in the row. It's white
now, but it was like the others then. *And if I
turn down that narrow lane where the tall chimney
shows over the trees I'll come to the dam.'*

Molly paused and I said, 'And did you?'

'Oh, yes. It was still there. The derelict mill
and its dam.' She shrugged. 'I did some
research. Local rag. I had the address, you see,
and the name. Raymond. All I had to do was
go back through the papers till I found the
story, and I found it. August 1922. Raymond
Lostock, nine. Death by misadventure. Buried
Hathersage cemetery, twenty-second of
August 1922.' She smiled. 'I've even visited
my grave.'

'You haven't?'

She chuckled. 'I have. So you see, you

found the right accomplice. Not through co-incidence of course. I don't believe in coincidence. No. We share a special gift and we found each other. It happens.'

'You mean . . . you'll help me, Molly?'

She grew serious. 'I have no reason to like your aunt, Kirsty. She sacked me the minute my illness started affecting my work, but that's not why I'm on your side. No. I'll do whatever I can because nobody should get away with murder. Trouble is, I'm not all that mobile nowadays. I don't know how . . .'

'You've helped already, Molly. More than you know.' I surprised myself by starting to cry. 'Just to know I'm not the only one. Not barmy. If I can come here sometimes, talk to you.'

'Of course you can, love. Any time. I've been alone too, you know. So alone.' She rose, crossed the space between us without her stick, toppled onto the sofa and wrapped her arms round me. I felt so safe in those arms, so *understood*, I wished I could snuggle for ever.

CHAPTER TWENTY-THREE

I got a bus back into town and walked home chanting,

Auntie Anne, Auntie Anne,
I'm gonna get you if I can

inside my head. I don't know where it came from. I certainly hadn't sat on the bus making it up. Maybe Grandma sent it. Anyway, I chanted it all the way home, in time with my footsteps. It was ten to five when I walked into the kitchen. Mum was fussing over a lasagne. 'Where've you been, Kirsty?' she said. 'Anywhere exciting?'

I nodded. 'Library, Mum. There was a shoot-out between bank robbers and librarians. They have it every Tuesday.'

'Really?' She spooned pasta sauce onto a layer of lasagne. 'Remind me to pop down there next week. I like a good shoot-out.'

She's dry, my mum. I wondered whether she'd act so cool if I told her I used to be her mother. I didn't think so. I reminded her she'd be teaching next Tuesday and went up to my room where I could think.

I'm gonna get you if I can. Big *if* though, isn't it?

CHAPTER TWENTY-FOUR

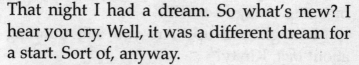

That night I had a dream. So what's new? I hear you cry. Well, it was a different dream for a start. Sort of, anyway.

I was confronting Auntie Anne. We stood face to face and I said, 'Where were you on the afternoon of June 13th 1983?'

'Why? It was before you were born.'

'I know, but it seems so real.'

'Nobody sees the past, dear. It's gone. Dead and gone.'

'A manager at twenty-two, then a murderer. Did you have people under you?'

'I had Molly. Oh, and a woman who cleaned the stairs three evenings a week.'

'Stairs? Which stairs, Auntie Anne?'

'The ones behind you.'

You can probably guess what happened

next. I glanced over my shoulder and saw we were standing at the top of a flight of stairs. Anne lunged forward and shoved me, and I toppled into the same old dream.

Next morning I waited till Dad went upstairs to shave, then said, 'Mum?'

'Yes, dear?' She was sweeping toast crumbs onto a plate with the edge of her hand.

'Did Auntie Anne *know* Grandma Elizabeth meant to change her will?'

Mum glanced up. 'Are you still thinking about *that*, Kirsty?'

'Yes.'

'But *why*, darling? It's ancient history.' She put the plate on the table and scrutinized my features. 'What exactly are you up to?'

I shook my head. 'I'm not up to anything, Mum. I'm interested, that's all.'

'You're a strange child,' she murmured. 'Always have been. But to answer your question – yes, Anne knew. Your grandma was the most open person I ever met. She'd never do anything in a hole-and-corner way. Having decided to alter her will, she sent for Anne and myself and told us.'

'Was Auntie Anne upset?'

'I don't think so. If she was she didn't show it.'

'*I* would've been. I mean, she could've sold the cottage for a lot of money, couldn't she?'

'She *did*, darling, after Grandma's accident. It went to some Arab gentleman with an unpronounceable name. I think your grandma knew Anne would sell the place and she wanted it to stay in the family, and that's why she decided to leave it to your dad and me. We'd have moved in, you see.'

I nodded. 'Hmm. It was sort of – *convenient* for Auntie Anne, wasn't it, Grandma having her accident just then?'

Mum frowned. 'You mustn't talk like that, Kirsty. Anne was devoted to your grandma. She was utterly devastated by the accident. It was weeks before she could hear it mentioned without breaking down. I'm sure she didn't see it as in any way convenient.'

'I'm sorry, Mum. I only meant—'

'I know what you meant, darling, and I didn't mean to snap at you.' She smiled ruefully. 'It has to be said my sister wasted no time disposing of the place, distraught as she was, once she had it, and nobody else ever saw a penny of the proceeds. Still . . .' She smiled again and stood up. 'It's all in the past now. Give me a hand with the dishes, there's a dear.'

All in the past. Dead and gone. That's what Auntie Anne thinks too, but she's mistaken. I'll give her 'utterly devastated' when I work out how to do it. By golly I will.

CHAPTER TWENTY-FIVE

Frighten her. Spook her. Get her so rattled she loses it completely. Blurts something in front of witnesses.

I was in my room, getting ready to go out. Sally Armitage had phoned. I was meeting her at Island. We'd have Cokes, then check out Our Price and the Body Shop and a few other places. Sally and I were at Cutler's Hill together. She's at Bessamer Comp now but we're still friends.

So here I sit, talking to my reflection in the mirror. Well, I can't talk to anybody else about it, can I? Except Molly, and she's not here.

How d'you spook someone? Well, there's all sorts of ways. I could hang something on Auntie Anne's front door – a white rooster with its throat cut. I saw that in a movie. Or I might make scary phone calls, talking into a hanky to disguise my voice. Then there's anonymous letters. I cocked an eye at the gorgeous creature in the glass. *That'*d be a good one to kick off with, Kirsty. An anonymous letter. Yeah.

We had a nice afternoon, Sally and me. She bought a box of those little coloured balls with bath oil in them, and I got Blur's new single. We chatted quite a bit, but I didn't mention my problem.

It was just after four when I got home. Mum and Dad had been tidying the rockery ready for winter. I went to my room, put Blur on and sat at the computer, trying to compose an anonymous letter. It's hard. Harder than you'd think. You've got to make sure you don't put anything in that might identify you, see? And I wanted it to be scary without being dead obvious. I mean, I didn't want to put, *I know you murdered your mother so admit it, you cow,* or anything like that. No. I was aiming at something a bit more subtle, with a touch of the supernatural. There's nothing like the supernatural for making someone feel uneasy. In the end I came up with this:

I'm gone, Anne. Dead and gone but I can't rest. And we know why, don't we, you and I? It's our little secret.

I was dead chuffed with it. I printed it out. One copy. And I *didn't* save it onto disk – I'm not *that* thick. I folded the printout neatly and put it in a very ordinary envelope, which I addressed in block capitals using my left hand. I'd meant to slip out and post it in the box on the corner but I realized I'd have to cadge a stamp off Mum, so instead I hid the thing under the carpet in my room. Tomorrow I'd buy a stamp a mile or two away and post it there. Can't be too careful when you set out to spook a killer.

CHAPTER TWENTY-SIX

So Thursday morning I left the house with the letter in an inside pocket of my jacket. I bought stamps at the main post office in town and posted it there. I wondered about fingerprints, but since Auntie Anne was hardly going to get the police in I reckoned I was safe. I thought of phoning Molly to let her know what I'd done, but decided to wait and see if my letter had any effect first.

Kids tend to use Island quite a lot and I felt like company, so I checked it out and it must've been my lucky day because Anna Buffham and Kylie Bickerdyke were there. We're not best friends or anything but we're in the same class at school and we get along OK. I got a Coke and walked over.

'Hi, Anna, Kylie. How's things?'

'Great. What you doing here, Kirsty?'

'Messing around.' I sat down. 'How about you?'

'Same. We're off looking at clothes when we've finished these.'

'I'll come with you.' I sipped my Coke. 'Done anything thrilling this week, then?'

'Certainly have,' enthused Kylie. 'I've been to Safeway with my mum – *twice*.'

'Twice!' I gasped. '*And* lived to tell the tale – I wish I had your guts, Kylie.' I looked at Anna. 'How about you?'

Anna leaned forward. 'Listen to this: we went to a garden centre Tuesday. Unarmed. Mum, Dad and me. Near the motorway. We bought bulbs in pots so we'll have hyacinths at Christmas.'

'Hyacinths at *Christmas*?' I goggled. 'Do you realize you can get four *years* for that, you reckless fool?'

'I know, and I don't care.' She eyed me. 'And you. What gut-wrenching stunts have you pulled so far?'

I'd have loved to tell them I was on the trail of a murderer, but of course I couldn't. Instead I leaned forward, cut my eyes this way and that and hissed, 'I posted a letter in broad daylight.'

'Who dares, wins,' murmured Kylie, and Anna laughed with a mouthful of Coke so it came down her nose. It was a daft morning but it took my mind off things. We split up at twelve and I walked home feeling pretty good. Better than Auntie Anne, I thought, when she opens tomorrow's post.

CHAPTER TWENTY-SEVEN

Well I can't tell you, can I? What happened when Auntie opened her letter, I mean. I wasn't there. We can imagine it though, if you like. Yeah – let's imagine it.

It's breakfast time. Uncle Brian's having kippers, same as always. If you've ever had kippers you'll know how they smell. It's a pong that gets everywhere. You can't get rid of it. Auntie Anne's what they call house-proud – mops and dusts and hoovers and polishes all day long, but you can always smell kippers when you walk in their place. I bet they've had a million rows about it.

Anyway, there they are, the pair of them. Him fiddling with his kippers, her nibbling toast with a sniffy look on her face, and they hear the post. 'Post,' says Anne, and Brian gets up to fetch it. It's just another morning in the life of a successful killer.

There are four items. He fans them out, walking back. There's an appeal from Oxfam, a bill, a business letter for him (he sells car phones) and mine, addressed in block capitals to his wife. 'Just the one for you, dear.' He drops it by her elbow, sits down and starts slitting envelopes with his butter knife.

Anne picks up her envelope, looks at it and frowns. Doesn't recognize the writing. Glances at the postmark. Yaxley. Somebody local then. She opens the envelope, extracts the neatly folded note, smooths it out, reads.

I'm gone, Anne. Dead and gone but I can't rest. And we know why, don't we, you and I? It's our little secret.

A small noise – a sharp intake of breath perhaps – causes Brian to look up. 'Something the matter?'

Anne swallows, shakes her head. 'No, no. Touched the cafetière with the back of my hand, that's all. Hot.'

'Hmm.' He goes back to his letter. Anne, heart pounding, reads the note again more slowly but there's no mistake. It reads as it did the first time, and there's no doubt in her mind what it's about. She refolds the thin paper, inhaling slowly in the hope that this might calm her, but her hands tremble as she returns the note to its envelope and slips it into the pocket of her smock. She can inhale slowly till she's blue in the face but it'll be a long, long time before Auntie Anne feels calm again. Her niece will see to that.

And her mother.

CHAPTER TWENTY-EIGHT

As it turned out, Auntie Anne wasn't the only one to get a shock that Friday morning. I came down to breakfast with a video playing inside my head of Anne opening my letter, and Mum said, 'Your dad and I have to be in school today, Kirsty. You know – setting up for the new half term, so I've phoned Auntie Anne and she'll do you some lunch.'

Terrific. Spook a killer, then go have lunch with her. I protested, trying to keep my voice from shaking. 'We don't need to bother Auntie Anne, Mum. I'm thirteen. I can get my own lunch.'

Mum shook her head. 'That's not the point, dear. We don't like the idea of leaving you in the house all day on your own. I *know* you think of yourself as grown up, but thirteen's not really that old, and you hear of such awful things happening these days. Your father and I will feel easier in our minds if we know some-one's keeping an eye on you.'

Yeah, right. I know what you mean, Mum. I'd feel much better knowing my kid was hav-ing lunch with someone who murdered her own mother. I didn't say this of course. I said, 'But Mum . . .'

'Kirsty!' Dad gazed at me over the top of his specs. 'Don't argue with your mother, please. Your aunt expects you at eleven o'clock, and you'll be there. Is that clear?'

I sighed. 'Yes, Dad.' It's terrific, having teachers for parents. Like being at a boarding school where there are no holidays.

'And don't be bothering Anne with your questions about Grandma Elizabeth,' put in Mum. 'She still gets upset.'

Yes, I thought but didn't say, and she's going to get a whole lot upsetter before I'm through.

So. I'd be arriving at my auntie's about three hours after my letter. Hairy end to half-term, or what?

CHAPTER TWENTY-NINE

I was dead nervous walking round to my auntie's. What if I hadn't been careful enough and she knew I sent the note? Or if she didn't know but mentioned it to me – would I blush and give myself away? I wished something would happen that'd give me an excuse not to go. A slight accident. Joe showing up for an unexpected visit. The start of World War Three.

Naturally none of these things happened, and at eleven o'clock precisely I knocked on the murderer's door.

'Come on in, dear – you're right on time.' She didn't sound delighted – tired would be nearer the mark. I followed her through, looking on every flat surface for my note. Needless to say it was nowhere in sight. In the spotless lounge she said, 'Lunch will be at half past twelve, dear. Would you like some coffee?'

'Uh – yes please, Auntie Anne.' I sat down, hoping I didn't look as nervous as I felt.

She brought a tray through and sat in the other chair. I watched her pour, looking for signs of tension. I didn't spot any. It was ten past eleven. I wondered what the heck we'd find to talk about till half twelve.

'Have you thought any more about a career, Kirsty?'

'Uh? Oh, no. No – I've decided not to bother till I'm about fifteen.'

'Absolutely right. Childhood's to be enjoyed, and it passes so very quickly. Have you heard from your brother lately?'

'Joe? No. He's not a letter writer. Mum watches the post, but she's nearly always disappointed.'

'Well.' Anne sipped her coffee. 'They say no news is good news.'

'Oh yes.' I nodded, looking at her over the rim of my cup. 'Better no letter at all than one with something bad in it.'

Something in her face. A flicker. I took a ginger biscuit. Nibbled. Anne's cup chattered a bit in its saucer. I looked across. Her hands were quivering ever so slightly. She saw I'd noticed and smiled ruefully. 'Nerves. Never give in to your nerves, Kirsty. I did. They've ruled me all my life.'

'I get twitchy too when something upsets me.' I smiled. 'It must be in the genes.' I looked at her. 'Are you upset about something, Auntie Anne?'

'Me? No. No – I'm a martyr to my nerves, that's all.'

I chuckled. 'Martyr. Funny – that's the second time I've heard that word today. Mum said *her* mother was a martyr to rheumatism.'

'Oh . . . did she? How did that come up, Kirsty?'

I shrugged. 'Mum felt a twinge, I think. She reckons it's hereditary.'

'Yes, well . . . I believe it is. And it's certainly true your grandma suffered with it. In fact it killed her, really.'

'Did it?' I gazed across at her. 'I thought it was a fall, Auntie Anne. Down some stairs.'

'Yes dear, it *was*, but you see the rheumatism made her unsteady on her feet and that's *why* she fell.'

'Ah.' I popped the last bit of biscuit in my mouth and chewed. 'What a sad way to die, Auntie Anne. Can't help your nerves much, thinking about that.'

'I – try *not* to think about it, Kirsty.'

I just bet you do, I thought. I didn't *say* it, of course. I just nodded, and a minute later she mumbled something about potatoes and went out to the kitchen. I stayed where I was, sipping coffee and feeling chuffed with myself. My Spook-Auntie-Anne campaign seemed to have got off to a promising start, *and* we were having steak and kidney pie for lunch.

I wonder if they get steak and kidney pie in prison?

CHAPTER THIRTY

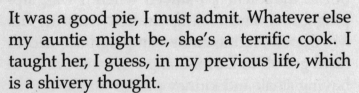

It was a good pie, I must admit. Whatever else my auntie might be, she's a terrific cook. I taught her, I guess, in my previous life, which is a shivery thought.

We didn't talk much over lunch. We never do. As I said before, I can't stand her and she senses it. Anyway, she'd be busy with her thoughts. I know *I* was.

OK, Sherlock – this was the first move. What's the second? She's rattled, but not to where she's about to confess. The thing to do is keep her reeling – give her no time to recover. But how?

Inspiration struck over pudding, only it wasn't inspiration so much as a sort of vision. There's this vase on Auntie Anne's sideboard. An art deco vase from the Twenties in yellow, green and red. It's been there years, but as my vacant stare alighted on it that lunchtime, I saw it somewhere else. I saw it on dusty floor-boards in a dim place that was crammed with junk. It only lasted a second, and as it faded I heard myself say, 'Why on *earth* did you rescue that horrid old thing from the Glory Hole, Anne?'

It wasn't me speaking. It wasn't. I wouldn't have dared call anything of Auntie Anne's horrid, especially in the circumstances. The words came out of my mouth but I wasn't responsible for them.

'What?' She paused, a forkful of glazed pear halfway to her lips. 'What was that you said, Kirsty?'

'N-nothing, Auntie Anne. I was – day-dreaming.'

She set down her fork. 'No you weren't. You said something about my vase. Something rude. And you mentioned . . . you said, "the Glory Hole". Sylvia – your mother – she's been talking about it, hasn't she? About the Glory Hole? What was she doing, eh? Sneering? About my lack of taste – was *that* it?'

'No!' I shook my head. I could see she was blazing mad and I was really scared. 'Nobody's

101

been sneering, Auntie Anne. Honestly. Not Mum. Not anybody. Why *should* they?'

'*Somebody*'s talked to you, Kirsty, or you wouldn't know about the Glory Hole, or that the vase was up there.'

'I . . . can't explain. I had a sort of daydream, that's all. I saw the vase on the floor. I *saw* it.' I could hardly get the words round the lump in my throat, and when I saw she didn't believe me I burst into tears.

She didn't comfort me. She wouldn't have, even if she'd not been mad. It isn't her way. She picked up her fork and set about demolishing her pear, leaving me to recover as best I might. The only good thing was, when I'd got a grip on myself and blown my nose and dabbed my eyes and all that, she didn't resume her interrogation, but we spent a ghastly afternoon all the same. I was glad when three o'clock crawled round and Dad showed up to drive me home.

Oh – there was one other good thing. All the time Auntie Anne was eating her pudding, her fork hand was shaking like mad.

CHAPTER THIRTY-ONE

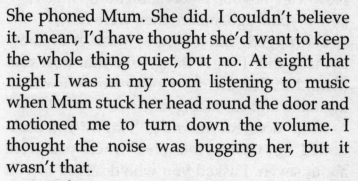

She phoned Mum. She did. I couldn't believe it. I mean, I'd have thought she'd want to keep the whole thing quiet, but no. At eight that night I was in my room listening to music when Mum stuck her head round the door and motioned me to turn down the volume. I thought the noise was bugging her, but it wasn't that.

'I've had your auntie on the phone,' she said. 'What happened at lunchtime, Kirsty? Anne tells me you made a remark about a vase. A rude remark. She practically accused me of talking to you about her behind her back.'

I shook my head. 'I wasn't rude, Mum. Not on purpose. I tried to explain to Auntie Anne but she wouldn't believe me.'

'Well.' Mum sat down on the bed. 'I think you'd better tell me what you told her, young woman.'

So I did, and she didn't believe me either. 'You *saw* the vase on the floor in Grandma's loft – is that what you're saying?'

I nodded.

'But how? How is that possible, Kirsty? How can anybody see something that happened years ago, before they were born?'

I shrugged. 'I don't know, Mum. All I know is that I did. I – get things like that now and then.' I pulled the chair away from the dressing table and sat facing her.

Mum nodded, frowning. 'I know. You mentioned the Glory Hole once when you were about seven. I asked you who'd talked to you about Grandma's attic and you said nobody. And once, when you were a baby, you pointed to your grandad in the snapshot on the sideboard and said "Bob", which was his name, though you couldn't possibly have known that then. You said it twice.' She shook her head. 'I don't know, Kirsty. Really I don't. You're a strange child.'

'I know I am.' Well – what *else* could I say,

short of blabbing the whole reincarnation thing?

Mum sighed. 'Well anyway, you must apologize to your auntie, Kirsty. Write her a note if you feel you can't face her, and let me see it before you seal the envelope.' She stood up. 'There's more than enough unhappiness in the world without families falling out.'

She was right of course. There is, but I couldn't see Auntie Anne being appeased by a written apology from me. Especially if it came on the same paper as that other note.

Hey, *that*'s an idea. I could make it part of my Spook-Auntie-Anne campaign.

CHAPTER THIRTY-TWO

I had a long think, then wrote this:

Dear Auntie Anne,

I'm writing to apologize for my behaviour on Friday. I didn't mean to call your vase horrid. It isn't horrid. In fact I've always liked it. I know I was rude, but I didn't lie to you. I do sometimes get funny turns when I seem to see bits of the past: you might remember the incident in Mr Newell's class I once told you about. I see other things too, most of them not very nice. So I really did see your vase on dusty floorboards but I shouldn't have said what I said, and I'm sorry. I hope you can forgive me.

Love,
Kirsty

I did it on the PC, printed it out and took it to Mum. She read it and looked at me. '*What* incident in Mr Newell's class, dear?'

'Tell you later, Mum. I can catch the last collection if I'm quick.' I hoped she might forget in the meantime. I used an envelope from the same pack, but this time I addressed it in my normal writing using my right hand. It was the same ballpoint though, and I *did* catch the collection, so my auntie would get it in the morning.

CHAPTER THIRTY-THREE

Next day was Saturday. Sally and I had fixed to meet at half ten at the coffee shop. I'd had my breakfast and was in my room getting ready when the phone rang and Dad yelled, 'Kirsty – phone!' I thought it was Sally to say she couldn't make it, but as he passed me the handset Dad whispered, 'Your Auntie Anne.'

I nearly died. I'd just been thinking about her. I swallowed and croaked, 'Auntie Anne?'

'Ah, Kirsty. I have your note. Thank you.'

'That's OK. I hope . . .'

'The thing is, it looks suspiciously similar to a note I received yesterday. Did you write that one as well, Kirsty?'

'No Auntie Anne, I didn't. I've only written the one, honestly. What was the other about?'

'Never you mind. Do your parents know about these – funny turns you mention?'

'No. Not really. I don't like to mention them in case they think I'm barmy. They know about the dream though, because I used to wake up screaming.'

'Dream? What dream, Kirsty?'

'This dream I've had since I was small. It's a nightmare. I'm at the top of some dark stairs and . . . something makes me fall. It's horrible.'

A silence followed this. I could almost *see* the colour draining from her cheeks. It was brilliant. After a bit she said, 'Yes, it must be absolutely dreadful. Do you . . . still get it?'

'Sometimes, but I don't scream any more. I guess I've got used to it.'

'Yes, but still . . . Anyway.' She injected some briskness into her voice. 'If you're absolutely sure you didn't write this other note, we'll say no more about it. Goodbye, Kirsty. Give my regards to your mum.'

'I will. 'Bye, Auntie Anne. And thanks.'

Bit of an abrupt end to our little talk but then she'd a lot to think about, and she wasn't the only one.

CHAPTER THIRTY-FOUR

I met Sally and we did the usual stuff. It didn't feel quite as good as last time because half-term was nearly over. 'School Monday,' she murmured, as we checked out the new singles at Our Price.

'Oooh, don't,' I moaned. 'Makes me poorly just thinking about it. Still . . .' I brightened a fraction, remembering. 'There's the Hallowe'en Rave to look forward to.' School was putting on this rave on the 31st, six-thirty till nine-thirty. They have it every year. It's the only good thing about Fettler's.

'Huh – all right for some. We never have owt like that up Bessamer. They don't know what a rave *is* at that dump.'

I chuckled. 'Talk to my dad. Maybe he'll run one.'

'Oh yeah – I can just see it.'

'Well – you should've come to Fettler's, same as me.'

'Didn't get the option, you turkey. Mum went to Bessamer so *I* had to go. Dunno why – it didn't exactly make a genius out of *her.*' She clucked disgustedly. 'Parents.'

I had a dream that night, and it wasn't my nightmare. There were two little girls in this dream. Sisters, seven or eight years old. One of them was heartbroken because the other had pinched her Barbie doll and sold it to some kid for a shilling. I was telling her off, really shouting, trying to make her cry but all she did was look back at me with an impudent expression, saying, 'Parents,' over and over in a scornful voice. As I yelled at her she spun the coin and caught it on the back of her left hand. 'Heads I win,' she murmured, 'tails you lose.' I was furious and tried to grab hold of her but I couldn't move. She turned away slowly, smiling, and that's when I woke up.

I know what you're thinking. The two little girls were Mum and Auntie Anne, right? Well that's what *I* thought, but the question was this: was it something that *really* happened – another of my flashbacks – or was it just a dream? I'd no idea, but what I did was write it down in my notebook, because if it *was* a glimpse into the past it might come in very handy for my Spook-Auntie-Anne campaign.

If I'd stopped to think, I might have realized the game I was playing was growing more deadly every day, but I didn't. I was too absorbed. If I'd been able to see into the near future as well as the distant past, I think I'd have dropped the whole thing.

CHAPTER THIRTY-FIVE

When it's wet I'm always dead early for school, because either Mum or Dad'll drop me off and they like to be at work by half eight. It was wet that Monday morning after the October break. I said goodbye to Mum and ran across the yard with my blazer over my head making for the covered area, and when I got there I had it to myself.

It was eight fifteen. I leaned on a pillar, watching raindrops falling like a bead curtain from the edge of the roof. A teacher's car came nosing through the gateway and swished by on its way to the parking area behind the main block, with old Baldock at the wheel. She's a Christian. Teaches RE. A sixth former told me she tries every year to get the Hallowe'en Rave stopped on the grounds that it's unchristian, yet she'll happily celebrate Diwali, Eid, Chanukah and Wesak. I wondered how she'd be on reincarnation.

Kids started drifting in at twenty-five past. Kylie Bickerdyke was on her bike as always. She parked it and came over. 'Hi, Kirsty. Great to be back, or what?' Rain beaded her glasses, made rat-tails of her hair.

'What,' I growled, and we laughed. She produced a crumpled Kleenex, whipped off her specs and started polishing them. A minute later Anna Buffham showed up. Her dad always dropped her off. 'Hi, Kylie, Kirsty. Good half-term?'

Kylie rehung her glasses and blinked at her friend. 'Not long enough. Roll on flippin' Christmas, I say.'

Anna nodded. 'Absolutely.'

'Baldock's abolishing it,' I told them. 'Unpagan.' That got a laugh, but actually I didn't feel like joking. Couldn't stop brooding over the Auntie Anne business. I'd started something that I had to finish somehow, but how? And when? Would it be over by Christmas, and if it was, what sort of Christmas would it be, with my auntie in jail and me responsible? Would Mum hate me? Anne was her sister, after all. And what about the other thing – me being Mum's mother? *That*'ll all come out, won't it? Bound to. And what then? Can it ever be the same between Mum and me? Can't see how. And the rotten thing is, I can't even talk to my friends about it.

There was one person I *could* talk to, though. Molly. I'd call her, lunchtime. From the box outside school. Fix to go see her. The buzzer sounded and I moved forward, merging with the throng, wishing I was one of them and one of them was me.

CHAPTER THIRTY-SIX

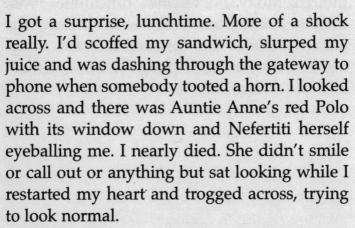

I got a surprise, lunchtime. More of a shock really. I'd scoffed my sandwich, slurped my juice and was dashing through the gateway to phone when somebody tooted a horn. I looked across and there was Auntie Anne's red Polo with its window down and Nefertiti herself eyeballing me. I nearly died. She didn't smile or call out or anything but sat looking while I restarted my heart and trogged across, trying to look normal.

'Auntie Anne ... what're *you* doing here?' Well – I had to say something, didn't I?

'I came hoping to see *you*, Kirsty. I expected to have to ask somebody to fetch you, but here you are. Where were you going, by the way?'

'Er – phone, Auntie Anne. I have to make a phone call.'

'Ah. Some boy, I suppose.' She still wasn't smiling. 'Well, never mind that now. Come round, get in. I want to show you something.'

My heart was battering my ribcage like it was trying to get out. I walked round the Polo. She leaned across, opened the door. I slid in.

'Look.' She thrust a sheet of paper at me. I took it, smoothed it in my lap. It was my note, but the first bit had been obliterated with Tipp-Ex. Now it read, *And we know why, don't we, you and I? It's our little secret.*

I swallowed, feeling my cheeks burn. 'Is this the other note you mentioned, Auntie Anne?' I knew it was, of course. God, was I scared.

'It certainly is. And now look.' She waved a second sheet in my face. It was my apology. 'Notice the similarities. Same paper, same spacing, same margins, same figure one at the foot. Same PC, I'd say.'

'No.' I shook my head again. 'This isn't mine, Auntie Anne. I told you – I only sent the one. I don't even know what this one *means*. And anyway it's been Tipp-Exed. I don't have Tipp-Ex.'

She scoffed. '*I* obliterated that line, Kirsty,

117

because it referred to something . . . personal. Highly personal. I think you wrote both notes.'

'But Auntie Anne – if I'd written this one I'd *know* what the first line said, wouldn't I? There'd be no point painting it out.' I reckoned that was pretty good, considering I was practically wetting my pants with terror.

She snorted. 'Very good, Kirsty. Very smart.' She jerked the note from my hand, screwed it up and shoved it in her bag. 'You don't fool me for one minute, girl, so don't think it. You're a child. A profoundly *disturbed* child if you ask me. You think you know something but you know nothing. Nothing.' She leaned across me and opened the door. 'Go make your phone call, and don't write me any more notes or I'll speak to your parents about getting help for you. Psychiatric help.'

I got out fast, I can tell you. Afterwards I wished I'd said something. Some parting shot, like, *It's* you *needs a shrink, Auntie Anne. A* prison *shrink maybe*, but I couldn't think of anything at the time, I was so rattled. I walked off shaking and after a minute she roared past, eyes front. If I'd needed to talk to Molly before, I certainly did now. By golly I did.

CHAPTER THIRTY-SEVEN

'Molly?'

'Yes . . . who's speaking?'

'It's me, Kirsty.'

'Oh – oh yes of course. How are you, Kirsty?'

'Not so good, Molly. That's why I'm calling. I'm . . . all mixed up. Don't know what to do.'

'Why, dear – has something happened?'

'No. Well . . . yes, a couple of things, but it isn't that. I just don't know whether I can . . . you know – turn my auntie in.'

'Hmm. Well Kirsty, I can't make that decision for you. It's really a family matter and I'm an outsider, but I will say this: to know a crime's been committed and not tell the police is a serious offence, even if the criminal is a relative. In other circumstances I'd say you had no choice, but since your suspicion arises out of dreams and memories of a previous life, you could remain silent on the grounds that it might all be nonsense, or that nobody would believe you if you *did* tell.'

'Yes.' Through the streaky glass wall of the phone box I could see kids trooping back to school. It was twenty to two. 'But you see, Molly, I'm *sure*. Absolutely sure. If I wasn't, I wouldn't have come to you in the first place. And there's something else.'

'I *thought* there was, because you're sounding distinctly shaky. You'd better tell me.'

'Well . . . I sent my auntie a note. An anonymous note. I was really careful, but she's linked it up with some other stuff . . . things I said, another note . . . and now she suspects me. She was here just now, outside school, waiting for me. I'm scared, Molly.'

'Hmm . . . dodgy, I'll admit. Well look – we can't really sort this out over the phone, Kirsty. Why don't you come up and see me – this evening if you're not too busy. And in the meantime I'll have a think and see if I can't come up with something that'll help. What d'you say?'

120

'I . . . yes, I'll come. I don't know what time exactly, but I'll come tonight. And thanks, Molly. I mean it.'

'I know you do, dear. I'll see you soon, then. 'Bye.'

''Bye, Molly.'

I hung up and walked back to school feeling a bit better. Only a bit, mind.

CHAPTER THIRTY-EIGHT

Molly gazed at me from her armchair. 'You're trying to make your aunt believe her mother's come back from the *grave*?'

'Yes. I thought that'd be the best way to make her confess. You know – scare her half to death.'

'Hmm.' She shook her head. 'As I recall, your aunt's the down-to-earth sort. Not the type to believe in ghosts, I wouldn't have thought. Still.' She sighed. 'You've started that way, so I suppose we're stuck with it. Well, all right. Look, why don't we fix it so your aunt gets an anonymous phone call from her mother when you're actually in her house? *That*'ll throw her off the scent, won't it?'

I looked at her. 'Well yes, it'd be absolutely

terrific, but why would I go to her house? I never go unless I have to.'

Molly smiled. 'Pretend you came to protest your innocence. We'll fix a time, and you knock on her door the very moment I'm reciting this little rhyme:

> *June thirteenth of '83.*
> *I didn't see you, but you saw me.'*

I gazed at her. 'That's *brilliant*, Molly, but it'll need exact timing. And what if Uncle Brian picks up?'

'I thought of that. If your uncle picks up I ask for Anne. If he says Anne's out I say, *When she gets back, recite this rhyme to her. She'll know who it was calling.* Then I say the rhyme. Whatever happens I'll be speaking as you're knocking. All we have to do is synchronize our watches. We'll do it *now*, this evening, if you like.'

And that's how I found myself creeping up a killer's path at one minute to nine on a dark, drizzly evening with my heart in my mouth, praying for the sound of a phone.

CHAPTER THIRTY-NINE

I loitered by the front door. There's a little panel of rippled glass in it. No light showed through the glass so the hallway, where the phone stood on a small table, was in darkness. I tried to look at my watch but there wasn't enough light. 'Come on, Molly,' I whispered. 'For Pete's sake come *on*.'

I nearly chickened out. I did. I was about three seconds away from scurrying down the path when the phone rang. God, talk about jump. I nearly died. Light showed through the glass as somebody opened a door inside, then the hall light came on and the ringing stopped and I heard Uncle Brian's voice. I took a deep breath and knocked.

'Anne!' I heard him call my aunt, and a second later his face appeared, distorted by the glass. I just had time to think, *Does he know about any of this – has Auntie Anne told him?* and then the door opened and there he was.

'Kirsty, at *this* time of night! It's after nine.'

'I know. I wanted a word with Auntie Anne.' I looked past him. She was standing with the handset to her ear, staring at me while she listened to Molly. You should have seen her face. 'I can see she's busy though. It'll do tomorrow.' Boy, did I want out of there! We'd fouled up, you see, Molly and me. Hadn't considered whether my uncle shared his wife's secret. It was crucial, I could see that now. If he knew nothing and I mentioned our lunchtime encounter in front of him, he was going to want to know what the heck it was all about. And if he *was* in on it, there'd be *two* of them after me instead of one.

'No, no.' He shook his head and stepped aside. 'Come on in, love. Your auntie won't be a minute.' He smiled. 'Can't be turning you away, can we, when you've come specially. What *would* you think of us, eh?'

I smiled and stepped inside because I had no choice. A line from a nursery rhyme went through my head as I followed him past my auntie and into the living room. *Won't you step into my parlour? said the spider to the fly*. It didn't help, I can tell you. I was like that fly, only worse.

Two spiders.

CHAPTER FORTY

'Tea, coffee?'

'Oh – coffee, please. No sugar.'

He smiled. 'Not watching your weight, surely. Not at thirteen.'

'Save me watching it later.' If there *is* any later, I added, but to myself.

'True.' He left the room as my auntie came in, looking pale. 'Not a word about ... you know,' she murmured, lowering herself into the armchair opposite mine, 'our little talk earlier. Your uncle knows nothing about it and I don't want him to.' She kept her voice low and an eye on the doorway. 'I – it seems I owe you an apology, Kirsty. I know now the note wasn't from you.'

I nodded. 'That's what I came to tell you,

Auntie Anne. That it wasn't from me.' I looked at her. 'How d'you . . . ?'

'Never mind. Your uncle's coming. So.' She adjusted her volume control as he appeared behind a loaded tray. 'You've decided university might be a better idea than plunging straight into the world of work, eh? I think you're very wise.' She looked at Uncle Brian as he set down the tray. 'Don't you think she's wise, darling?'

My uncle nodded. 'I'm sure she is, my dear.' He grinned ruefully. 'What I *don't* understand is why our wise niece felt compelled to communicate her decision to you at nine o'clock at night when it'll be – what – five years before she actually starts university.' He was joking, but my auntie explained anyway.

'Ah, well, you see, Kirsty came to see me the other day about her future.' She chuckled. 'Apparently they start asking pretty early on at school what their pupils want to do with their lives. Anyway we talked, and I suppose I must have put Kirsty off the idea of work at sixteen, hence her decision. Anyway, nine o'clock's not *that* late. The poor girl'll think she's not welcome if you keep going on about the time.'

128

'No no!' He shook his head. 'I didn't mean . . .' He looked at me. 'You know I didn't mean *that*, don't you, Kirsty? You're welcome any time at this house. Any time at all.'

I nodded, wanting only to be gone. 'I know, and I wouldn't have come, only I was passing on my way home and I thought . . .'

He nodded. 'Quite right too. Ignore the geriatric grousings of your miserable old uncle and drink your coffee while it's hot.' He turned to Auntie Anne. 'Who was that on the phone, by the way? Didn't recognize the voice.'

'Pooh! Some woman selling insurance, that's all. Damned cheek. I let her rattle on a bit, then hung up without speaking. Only way to deal with that sort of thing.'

Smooth liar under pressure, my Auntie Anne. Takes after her 'mother', you might say.

CHAPTER FORTY-ONE

So Molly's plan worked perfectly: my auntie thinks her dead mother's composing when she should be *de*composing and I'm in the clear, right?

Well, I dunno. She's vain and snobby and she murdered her own mother, but Auntie Anne's not thick. It'd be dangerous to underestimate her.

I'd learned one interesting thing though. Uncle Brian wasn't in on his wife's dark secret. I couldn't decide whether that was going to make things easier or harder.

'And where have you been, young woman?' goes Dad. Head of English and he starts a sentence with 'And'.

'Sally's.'

'Till *this* time?'

'No, Dad. Till a quarter of an hour ago, then there's the walk home.'

'Yes, and that's the bit your mother and I don't like, Kirsty. The walk home. Have you any idea how many young women are murdered, walking home?'

'No, Dad. Have you?'

'Too many, that's how many. Nine o'clock's far too late for a girl to be out alone. In future we want you to phone if you're going to be late, and one of us will come and pick you up.'

Great. I *told* you it's wonderful having teachers for parents, didn't I? Anyway, I didn't argue. I'd just had a brill idea for my next note and I couldn't wait to try it out.

CHAPTER FORTY-TWO

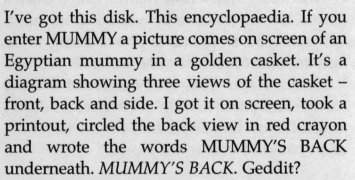

I've got this disk. This encyclopaedia. If you enter MUMMY a picture comes on screen of an Egyptian mummy in a golden casket. It's a diagram showing three views of the casket – front, back and side. I got it on screen, took a printout, circled the back view in red crayon and wrote the words MUMMY'S BACK underneath. *MUMMY'S BACK.* Geddit?

I folded the printout, shoved it in an envelope and addressed it to Auntie Anne. I could hardly write for giggling. MUMMY'S BACK. You've got to admit it's *really* funny. I had stamps left from when I posted the first note, so I stuck one on and hid the envelope in the bag I use for school.

I'd just finished when I remembered the dream I'd had about the two little girls.

Remember? One had sold the other's doll, but I had no way of knowing whether it really happened? Well, I decided to take a chance. Trust my dream. After all, my dreams had proved pretty accurate up to now and the computer was on, so I might as well do a note. I wrote this:

Remember when you sold your sister's doll, Anne? I do. I ought to have known then you were far too fond of money.

I printed it out and closed straight away without saving. Wouldn't do for Mum to walk in and see *that* on screen. Another envelope, another stamp, and then all I had to decide was which to post first, doll or mummy.

No contest.

CHAPTER FORTY-THREE

I dreamed a scary dream. Not the stairs. That one wasn't coming much any more. In this dream it was night and I was walking in a dark, lonely place. There were buildings of some sort but nobody was in them, and there were like high hedges on both sides which I couldn't see over. There was a glow in the sky ahead of me and I was walking towards it, but it was quite far away. I was trying to hurry – I was frightened – but something loose I was wearing kept catching on the hedge and I had to keep stopping to free myself. I'd just done this for the umpteenth time when a figure stepped out of the bushes in front of me. It was silhouetted against the glow so I couldn't see its face. I didn't recognize the person but there was an overwhelming sense of menace, and as whoever it was drew near I screamed and woke up. My heart was thumping like mad and it was ages before I nodded off again.

I posted MUMMY'S BACK next morning on my way to school. It wasn't raining so I walked, taking the short cut through the allotments which brings you out on the school's all-weather pitch. We're not supposed to come that way – there's a school rule against it, plus the allotment holders don't like it, but it cuts off a big corner and gets you away from the traffic. Loads of kids use it.

It was an ordinary Tuesday at school. All the routine stuff, but I managed to liven it up for myself by imagining the postman emptying the box, dropping my envelope in his bag, and Auntie Anne opening it tomorrow morning. It'd certainly take her mind off the smell of kippers for a minute or two.

CHAPTER FORTY-FOUR

First period Wednesday morning we had RE with old Baldock. We were doing the spread of Buddhism, and Baldock was explaining how bits of earlier religions got mixed in with Buddhism as it spread, altering it in various ways so that now there were various schools of Buddhism, though they all had the same basic beliefs.

'Something similar happened to Christianity,' she said, 'as it seeped into northern Europe, so that we celebrate Easter with decorated eggs and Christmas with mistletoe, holly and other evergreen boughs. These are remnants of paganism, sometimes called the "old religion".'

'What about Hallowe'en, Miss?' This from Anthony Yallop, the class clown. Everybody knew how old Baldock felt about Hallowe'en. With a bit of luck Anthony's question would divert her till the buzzer.

'Hallowe'en.' She said it like you might say 'Doggy poo' – distaste warping her mouth. 'Hallowe'en actually means holy evening, Anthony. It's the eve of All Hallows, or All Saints' Day, but it falls on the same day as an earlier, pagan festival to do with witches and hobgoblins and so forth and its Christian significance is now buried under a commercially generated avalanche of the symbols of gross superstition.'

'Yeah, but like,' pursued Anthony, 'it means that when we have the Hallowe'en Rave a week tomorrow we'll *really* be celebrating a Christian festival?'

Baldock shook her head. 'Not dolled up as witches and warlocks you won't. Not with pumpkin lanterns and broomsticks and masks. Not with bats and cats and spiders and whatnot. Nothing remotely Christian about any of that, I can assure you.'

'But, Miss . . .' The boy puckered his brow. 'If it's OK to have Easter eggs, and Christmas trees and all that even though *they're* pagan, what's wrong with having pagan stuff at Hallowe'en? I don't get it.'

He did a great job, old Yallop. Kept Baldock busy for twenty-five minutes and wound her up into the bargain. As a practising Christian she's supposed to be gentle and mild but you could see her struggling to control herself. It was brilliant. Three hundred years ago she'd have burned him at the stake.

It was breaktime before I remembered Auntie Anne. MUMMY'S BACK. Gross superstition of course, but all the same it'd prey on her mind, and I'd be slipping along to the post-box with my second note at lunchtime. Talk about piling it on.

Chapter Forty-five

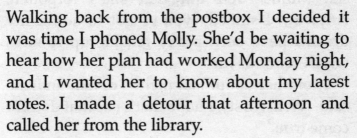

Walking back from the postbox I decided it was time I phoned Molly. She'd be waiting to hear how her plan had worked Monday night, and I wanted her to know about my latest notes. I made a detour that afternoon and called her from the library.

'Molly?'

'Kirsty. Are you all right? I've been worried.'

'Sorry. I guess I should have called yesterday. I'm fine. Your plan worked like magic. Auntie Anne looked as if she'd seen a ghost, and she actually apologized for having suspected me.'

'That's good. You *will* be careful though, dear, won't you? It's a dangerous game we're playing.'

'I know, Molly, and I *am* being careful. I've posted two more notes.' I told her about them. She chuckled over MUMMY'S BACK but thought the other a bit dodgy. 'What if your dream wasn't about Anne, Kirsty? What if it wasn't about real people at all?'

'Well,' I countered, 'if it wasn't about her she'll be mystified. Maybe she'll think she *did* sell Mum's doll but that she's forgotten. Anyway,' I smiled, 'you've got to admit my dreams have been pretty reliable up to now, which reminds me.'

I told her about last night's dream and she said, 'Well, Kirsty, I hope that's *one* that doesn't come true.'

I laughed. 'No chance, Molly. That one *was* just a dream.'

Neither of my parents was home when I got in, so I didn't have to explain why I was late. I peeled some spuds and got green beans and pizzas from the freezer. We eat a lot of convenience foods at our house, especially when I'm first home. When I'd got everything started I went up to my room to work on my witch's outfit for the Hallowe'en Rave. I'd cadged three metres of fine black nylon net from Grandma Kath. There's a prize for the best costume, and this year it's going to be mine.

CHAPTER FORTY-SIX

I *am* being careful. That's what I'd told Molly, but I hadn't been careful enough. As I sat on the bed putting lace and satin together to make a witch's dress, Auntie Anne was busy putting two and two together to make four, though of course I didn't know this at the time.

It was the stamps. I'd bought a book of four the day I posted the first note. You know – *I'm gone, Anne.* That one. I'd used two of the stamps on that and my note of apology, and the other two on MUMMY'S BACK and the doll note, but in tearing out the second stamp I'd been careless. I didn't notice at the time that it hadn't torn cleanly along the perforation but had lost a corner. It was just a tiny corner, left attached to the next stamp, but I'd stuck that one on MUMMY'S BACK, so Auntie Anne ended up with both stamps. Now I've said she wasn't thick and she wasn't. She'd hung on to the envelope with the incomplete stamp, and when she got the one with the extra bit she compared them. The extra bit on MUMMY'S BACK fitted exactly the missing corner on my apology and bingo! She had me cold.

If I'd known, I wouldn't have sat there sewing a flipping witch outfit, I can tell you. What I can't tell you is what I'd have done instead. Died, probably.

CHAPTER FORTY-SEVEN

I don't know what I expected my two notes to do, but whatever it was I was doomed to disappointment. Nothing happened at all. Or perhaps I should say nothing *seemed* to happen. In fact, having proved herself a better detective than I was, Auntie Anne was planning a showdown, but that's for later. In the meantime my life went on as normal, or as near normal as it has ever been.

Thursday, the talk at school was all about the Hallowe'en Rave, now a week away. Anthony Yallop claimed he intended coming as Irene Baldock, complete with cross and Bible. 'I'll be by the door,' he told us, 'cursing all you sad pagan plonkers as you go in.'

'You wouldn't dare,' taunted Kylie. 'Old Swanny'd suspend you for a month or expel you, and anyway you couldn't make the costume. Boys' costumes are always rubbish.'

'Not this one,' rejoined Anthony. 'It's a dress my gran wore about seventy years ago so it's just like the stuff Baldock trolls around in. Only one snag – I'm too good-looking.'

'Hooo!' cried Maureen Crossley. 'You're about as good-looking as a bagful of chisels, you tube. In fact if I had to choose, I'd go for the chisels every time.'

There was more like that. Everybody was making an outfit. Everybody hoped to take the prize, which this year was a CD ROM software package. I kept quiet about my own effort, which I believed was good enough to win.

Sally phoned at teatime, inviting me round. The wrinklies let me go by myself but Dad insisted on picking me up after. It was a good evening. We talked and listened to music and Sally's mum sent out for a pizza. I didn't mention the rave because I knew Sally envied us Fettler's kids, and at half nine Dad showed up to drive me home. Sally stood on the step, waving. I waved back, blissfully ignorant of the awful thing that was to happen before I'd see her again.

145

CHAPTER FORTY-EIGHT

So that was Thursday. Friday slipped by, then Saturday, without a murmur from Auntie Anne. It was sort of spooky, waiting for something to happen. Wondering how long I should give it before trying something else.

To be absolutely honest I was getting fed up with the whole thing. I mean, excitement's OK in small doses but it starts to get to you after a while. You're tense all the time. Can't relax. You know – have I given myself away? What if she's waiting when I come out of school? What if she's phoned Mum? Molly's warning kept replaying inside my skull: *It's a dangerous game we're playing*.

A dangerous game, yes, and one I couldn't just choose to abandon. You know about a murder, I kept telling myself. A *murder*. You can't ignore a thing like that, even when it's your auntie. You can't walk away from it. The game's on and you've no choice but to play to the end, even though it doesn't feel like a game any more.

Sunday morning I phoned Molly. From a box of course. She said, 'I keep thinking about that dream you told me. It worries me.'

'What dream?'

'You know – the one where you're walking in a lonely place and somebody—'

'Oh, *that*. That's nothing to worry about, Molly. I told you. That was just a dream.'

'Ah, well I'm not so sure, love. Your dreams . . .'

'Look. I don't walk in lonely places, right? Chance'd be a fine thing, with Dad insisting on picking me up wherever I go. No – what I'm phoning about is . . .' I told her there'd been no response to my latest notes. She said, 'What d'you *expect*, Kirsty? My anonymous phone call threw her off your scent. She'll be driving herself crazy trying to figure out who her persecutor is, now that you're in the clear. Why would *you* hear anything?'

147

I felt better when she said that. She's got her head screwed on, old Molly. When I asked her if she thought I should give Anne another poke she said, 'No, not yet. Leave it a while. Your auntie's pretty frightened, Kirsty, and frightened people have been known to confess, just so they don't have to go on being frightened. So leave it. Take a break. Concentrate on getting ready for Hallowe'en and when it comes, enjoy it.'

Good old Molly. I was glad I phoned her. Really glad.

CHAPTER FORTY-NINE

Monday breakfast Mum said, '*What* incident in Mr Newell's class, dear?'

'Huh?'

'You know – you mentioned it in your letter of apology to Auntie Anne a week last Friday. Said you'd tell me later.'

'Oh, *that*.' Memory like a flipping elephant, my mum. I told her about the siren and my trance, if that's what it was, all those years ago. Dad was doing some last minute preparation so he wasn't there to hear. When I'd finished, Mum sighed.

'That's very strange, Kirsty. It certainly sounds as though you were given a glimpse into the past, but since that's not possible I'm inclined to agree with your auntie that the whole thing must have arisen in your imagination. Anyway' – she gazed at me – 'I think you ought to stop worrying about things that happened a long time ago, Kirsty, and concentrate on the present. And the future, of course. The past is the past but the future is *yours*.' She smiled. 'How's the costume coming along?'

'It's OK.'

'Good. The thing is, neither Dad nor I will be home Thursday teatime. Another of those interminable meetings, so I'm afraid you'll have to go to your auntie's for tea.'

'No!' I shook my head. 'No, Mum, I can't. Not Thursday. It'd mean carrying my outfit about all day in my bag, ruining it. Let me have a key, Mum, *please*. I'll get my own tea, change and go back to school at six thirty. I'll be OK, honestly. Let me, Mum. Just this once.'

Mum pulled a face. 'I don't know, Kirsty. Your dad—'

'You can persuade him, Mum. I *know* you can.'

'I'm not so sure. And he'd certainly insist on collecting you when this – rave's over. What time's it due to finish, by the way?'

'Half nine, and I don't mind being collected

150

if only I don't have to set off from my auntie's. Oh *please*, Mum.'

She sighed. 'All right, dear, I'll see what I can do.'

'Oh *thanks*, Mum. I mean it.'

I *did* mean it. Tea with Nefertiti, Thursday of all days? It'd have wrecked the whole thing for me.

CHAPTER FIFTY

It's always a drag going to school. Goes without saying, but that Monday morning felt especially bad. I wasn't sure why at the time, but I know now. I'd only done a half-term at Fettler's, but half a term had been long enough to show me the difference between primary and upper school. Back at Cutler's Hill the coming weeks would be enlivened by a number of events and activities leading right up to Christmas. Like, today they'd probably start making Hallowe'en masks and witch mobiles and covering the classroom walls with spooky pictures. They'd learn a Hallowe'en song and write witchy poems and stories. They'd have a *week* of Hallowe'en, not just an evening like us. And as soon as Hallowe'en's over, Bonfire

Night looms, so off they'd go making guys and bonfire scenes in collage and doing an assembly about taking care with fireworks. Then, before the ashes have cooled in the grey remains of bonfire heaps it's time to start learning carols and rehearsing the Christmas Concert and before you know it it's the holidays again.

Well, that's the way to do it if you ask me, but it doesn't happen at Fettler's. No chance. It's all revision here. Revision, tests and homework. Luckier than Sally Armitage up at Bessamer, but still.

Anyway, as I was wending my merry way through the allotments towards the all-weather pitch, breaking the school rule, Mum was talking to Auntie Anne on the phone. Unbeknown to me, she'd asked her sister to give me tea on Thursday before she'd mentioned the matter to me and now, having persuaded Dad to let me be home alone, she was cancelling the arrangement. Needless to say this was not breaking my auntie's heart, but it *was* telling her I'd be all by myself Thursday teatime, which happened to fit in perfectly with a plan she'd been hatching ever since she'd matched my two stamps. So in trying to do me a favour, Mum was actually setting me up for the worst encounter of my life. So thanks a bunch, Mum. I love you anyway, you know that.

CHAPTER FIFTY-ONE

But anyway, things carried on in their usual boring way till Thursday morning when Miss Perrigo and her sixth form drama group started transforming the sports hall ready for the rave. Apparently they did something similar every year, but to us first year kids it was unbelievable. At break we stood gobsmacked as these seventeen- and eighteen-year-olds came staggering across the yard from the art block carrying the flats they'd knocked up out of four-by-twos and canvas. These flats were painted to look like sections of cave wall complete with fissures, slime and cobwebs. While one crew was erecting the flats all around the walls, another was busy on top of a mobile scaffold hanging spiders, bats and polystyrene stalactites from the roof. Miss Perrigo's area of expertise was lighting, and a mob under her was fixing great lamps onto gantries and running what looked like miles of cable down the walls and along the floor behind the flats. The buzzer went long before the job was done and we had to tear ourselves away, but you could tell it was going to be brilliant.

By lunchtime the hall was unrecognizable. We stood exclaiming round the main doors till this sixth-form prefect, Mossman, came and shifted us. 'You're in the way, you twisted pygmies!' she yelled. 'It'll all be here tonight, and you can gawp then till your nasty little eyes drop out. In the meantime get back behind the bike sheds, pick your noses and pretend it's just another day.' Terrific role model, old Mossman. I want to be just like her when I'm seventeen.

At hometime I came out of the cloakroom with Anna Buffham and Kylie Bickerdyke and there in the yard was a beat-up Transit in yellow and purple with MOBY DISK in white on the side.

'What the heck's that?' cried Anna.

'Sounds, you moron,' growled a passing year ten. 'For tonight.'

'You mean, there's a professional disc jockey?'

''Course. You're not in kid-school now, you know.' He jerked his head towards a knot of sixth-form girls round the sports-hall doors, which were closed. 'Simon flippin' Warner fan club, see?'

'How d'you mean?' asked Kylie, but the boy was striding away.

'Simon Warner,' said Anna. 'Our Steph talks about him. Reckons he's dead sexy.' Steph is Anna's big sister. She works at Marks and Spencer and goes to clubs all the time. 'Let's go over.'

A red-haired sixth-former with a fine crop of zits glowered at us. 'What do you kids want?'

'Same as you,' chirped Kylie. 'See Simon Warner.'

'Huh!' The redhead sneered. 'Simon's a man, not a teddy bear. He doesn't want little kids gawping at him.'

Kylie eyed the closed doors. 'Not exactly breaking the doors down to get to *you*, is he?' she growled. 'Pizza-face.'

You could tell this girl was sensitive about her complexion by the way she chased us halfway down the road. Kylie'd had to leave her bike behind. 'I don't care,' she gasped, when we'd finally shaken off our enraged pursuer. 'Don't need it tonight anyway. Not with my outfit.'

Anna looked at her. 'Coming by broomstick, are you?' We laughed, but I'd be laughing on the other side of my face in three hours' time. By golly I would.

CHAPTER FIFTY-TWO

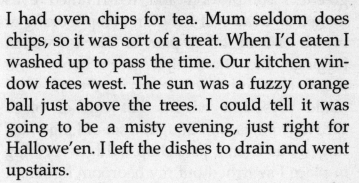

I had oven chips for tea. Mum seldom does chips, so it was sort of a treat. When I'd eaten I washed up to pass the time. Our kitchen window faces west. The sun was a fuzzy orange ball just above the trees. I could tell it was going to be a misty evening, just right for Hallowe'en. I left the dishes to drain and went upstairs.

I've got this eye make-up. Green, like the stuff my auntie uses. I washed, then did my whole face with it – cheeks, forehead, all round my nose and mouth. I did my lips blue and rubbed red lipstick on my eyelids with my little finger. Then I gave myself plenty of wrinkles with an eyebrow pencil and sprayed my tatty hair before standing back from the mirror to gauge the overall effect. It was wicked, though I say it myself.

Now for the costume. I'd taken an old black dress of Mum's, hacked it all round the hem and tacked on Grandma Kath's net so it sort of swirled round my shoulders and formed a close-fitting hood with a veil I could pull down over my face. Behind the veil my wrinkled, greenish complexion and red-rimmed eyes looked so dead real I couldn't stop looking at myself. I had on a pair of black woollen leggings and these high green boots with pointy toes and little buttons up the sides. I'd made myself a witch's hat out of black cartridge paper and bought a set of long black fingernails from a joke shop. With everything in place I switched out my bedroom light and damn near screamed when I saw my reflection in the mirror. That software was as good as mine.

The sun had set but it was only ten to six. I didn't dare sit down for fear of crushing Grandma's net so I went downstairs and wandered from room to room, watching the clock. Funny how time drags when you're wanting it to fly.

By five past six I'd had enough. 'What's wrong with arriving a bit early?' I whispered. I let myself out, hoping none of the neighbours would see me but since it was almost dark and the mist had thickened there was little chance of that. What I didn't know was that Auntie Anne had just set off in her car with the intention of catching me at home. So I set off, hoping to meet some little trick-or-treaters I could scare the pants off, but there was nobody about. I didn't fancy making a spectacle of myself along the main road, so I hung a left and headed for the allotments. It was strictly against the rules and Dad would've had a fit but witches don't give a toss about that stuff. It wasn't till I was in there among the unkempt privet hedges and narrow muddy paths that I recognized the landscape of my dream.

CHAPTER FIFTY-THREE

You know which dream. Walking in a dark, lonely place. The one I told Molly was just a dream. Well here it all was, complete with hedges to snag my costume and the distant glow in the sky which was the floodlights on the all-weather pitch, switched on for the benefit of parents dropping their kids off in the fog.

As soon as it hit me I turned back. I did. You probably think I was being daft but *you* weren't there. You weren't *me*. Anyway, I started hurrying back the way I'd come, or trying to, but the net round my shoulders was catching on the privet. I had to keep stopping to free myself. You can bet I was scared. Really scared. It was all so like my dream that when Auntie Anne stepped out in front of me I wasn't even surprised.

I screamed though, I don't mind admitting it. Come face to face with a murderer in a lonely spot and you'd scream too. I tried to run, caught my foot in something, crashed through some privet and found myself backed up against a derelict greenhouse with Auntie Anne's hand clamped over my mouth. I struggled to tear myself away but she was leaning on me, pressing me into the crumbling brick. A crazy thought went through my mind. *Careful, you'll crush my outfit*. Here I was about to die, and some part of me was still after that software.

She was talking to me, hissing in my face. 'Listen. Stop fighting and listen to me, you stupid child.' I didn't stop. I knew I was fighting for my life. I grabbed her arm with both hands and tried to jerk it clear of my mouth so I could scream. The road was only yards away. People'd be passing. If I could just cry out someone was bound to hear, but she was strong. You wouldn't believe how strong she was. I tried to bite her hand but I couldn't find anything with my teeth, and then she punched me in the stomach. It was like being hit by a big bloke. The pain was unbelievable. I couldn't breathe. I wanted to double up but she was holding me and hissing in my face, something about a flipping doll. I was gasping and crying, plastering her hand with tears and snot. She was *killing* me, for Pete's sake. What had *dolls* to do with it?

Dolls. My dream. Two little girls. *The wrong way round,* she was saying. *You got it the wrong way round.* I knew then what she was on about, and she must have seen it in my eyes because she unclamped my mouth enough so I could choke out, 'What?'

'She sold *my* doll, Kirsty. Your mother sold *my* doll. She was like that.'

'Mum?' I gazed at her through my tears, shaking my head. The paper hat had slipped off and was on the ground. I felt it crackle under my boot. 'No she wasn't. Isn't. *You* are, and you're a murderer too. You pushed Grandma Elizabeth downstairs. I *know* you did.' My voice had risen. I screamed the words in her face till she clamped her hand over my mouth again. She was shaking her head.

'Wrong again, Kirsty, and it's no use screaming at me. You started this. You insisted on stirring up the past. You thought you knew the truth but you didn't, and now you *have* to know and you won't like it. You see, Kirsty, it was your *mother* who pushed your grandma down those stairs.'

'No!' I jerked my head from side to side against the pressure of her hand. 'You're lying. You must think I'm stupid. Mum could never do a thing like that. She's kind. Not like . . .'

'Not like me? Not like your wicked Auntie Anne?' she scoffed. 'Listen, Kirsty. Stop struggling and listen.' She removed her hand from my mouth. 'I'm not going to hurt you. Not physically. Any hurt you *do* feel you've brought on yourself by snooping.' She glanced about her. 'I wouldn't have chosen to do this here, Kirsty. I tried to catch you at home but you'd left, so this'll have to do. When I arrived at your grandma's house on June thirteenth 1983, your mother was already there and *my* mother was lying at the foot of the stairs. I'd caught her in the act, you see. My kind sister. She assumed poor Mother had altered her will as she'd said she would, but she hadn't. I knew that because I was in the habit of dropping in on her practically every day. Your mother hardly ever called, so she didn't know.'

'Why?' I gasped. I was bent forward, my arms wrapped round my stomach. I felt so sick and was trembling so badly I almost fell down. 'Why would Mum want to kill Grandma if the cottage was going to be hers anyway? It doesn't make sense.'

My aunt shook her head. 'No it doesn't, and it's no use asking me why she did it. Ask *her*.'

I shook my head. 'No. I don't believe you. *You* had a reason. You did it. You're just trying to get out of it.'

She sighed. 'If I did it – if it *was* me, Kirsty, why am I wasting my time talking? Why don't I strangle you and creep away before somebody shows up?' She shook her head. 'No, Kirsty. It wasn't me. I didn't deserve those notes. Those cruel notes. "Mummy's back".' She spat the words. 'Did you really imagine you could frighten me with superstitious nonsense like—'

It was then we both saw her, silhouetted against the glow. Grandma Elizabeth on her two sticks, hobbling towards us along the muddy path. 'Mummy's back,' she croaked.

CHAPTER FIFTY-FOUR

With a hiss of indrawn breath my auntie took a step backwards, staring at the oncoming figure. A whimpering sound began which I realized was coming from me. As the hobbling woman drew near, the silhouette effect began to break down. Features became discernible. Black pits where eyes might be. The pale blade of a nose. A glint of teeth. I'd never seen my grandma of course, but this face seemed strangely familiar. Three more tottering steps and I had it. 'Molly!' I cried. 'How'd *you* get here?'

Instead of answering, Molly said, 'Get away from that child, Anne Tasker. If you've hurt her I'll . . .'

'Molly Barraclough.' Auntie Anne was trying to sound like she knew all the time but the silhouette had had her going, same as me. My heart was still thumping. 'Of course. I *thought* I recognized that voice on the phone.' She sneered at Molly. 'You fool, you've got it totally wrong, which shouldn't surprise me since you messed up practically everything you touched at Whiteleys. My sister Sylvia, remember? 'Course you do. Good, kind Sylvia. Well *she*'s the one you're after, the pair of you. *She* killed our mother. I'm just an accessory after the fact or whatever they call it, so you go right ahead. Tell the police.' She laughed briefly. 'You'll be doing me a favour, because to tell you the truth I'm sick and tired of guarding my sister's dirty secret.'

We went back to my place, the three of us, and waited for Mum to come home. I don't know how long it was because I was practically out of my mind. I remember running upstairs, tearing off my precious costume and rubbing and rubbing at the green on my face, believing that if I could just look myself again everything would be all right. After a bit Molly dragged herself up the stairs and made me put on jeans and a jumper and come down. She'd made tea. Or maybe that was Auntie Anne.

Anyway, Molly gave me a cup and I suppose I drank it, but I honestly don't remember, my head was so messed up. One part of me wanted my mum, another part hoped she'd never come. When I heard the car in the driveway I jumped up, ran upstairs and slammed my door. I heard Mum and Dad in the hallway. Dad laughed at something. These were the final seconds of their normal life and they didn't know. They didn't even *know*. I flung myself on the bed and wrapped the pillow round my ears so I wouldn't hear the voices which were about to wreck our lives. To make absolutely sure I wouldn't hear, I started singing very loudly a song they taught us at Cutler's Hill. A Hallowe'en song:

> *When stars appear and children sleep*
> *And witches round their cauldrons creep*
> *And Jack-o-Lanterns walk the night*
> *And bats and demons take to flight . . .*

Maybe you know it. Anyway, I lay curled on my side with the pillow round my head belting this out at the top of my voice, and I didn't stop when someone came in ages later and tried to pull the pillow away. I clung on to that pillow and kept on singing, even when two women I'd never seen before got me up and half-carried me downstairs and out to the ambulance. I remember the flashing blue light.

CHAPTER FIFTY-FIVE

Mum gave herself up to the police. Well, three people knew her secret now and anyway she was sick of it. Sick of living with her conscience. I mean, just think what my night-mares must have done to her for a start. My little flashbacks.

I was four days in hospital, sedated. They sedated Dad too, at home, and they wouldn't let me anywhere near the court when Mum's case was heard.

Oh, it's OK. It was a few years ago. We're over it, I guess. As over as we'll ever be. She was in this open prison in Cheshire. Not a bad place, considering. We visited monthly, Dad and I. Sometimes Joe came too. He's a psychologist now and works at a prison, though not that one. He says people do bad things for all sorts of complicated reasons and we must try not to judge them.

I don't judge Mum. No way. I didn't know till Dad told me, but at the time she did what she did she was under a lot of pressure. They weren't living in the house I grew up in. They were poor, just out of college, living in a rotten, damp flat that had mice and was making Joe poorly. They were desperate to move but they couldn't afford anything right then. One day, listening to Joe cough and cough, Mum just snapped. She knew her mother's cottage was coming to her eventually but she needed it now. *Now*, for her baby's sake. She went out there with little Joe coughing and wheezing on her back. She didn't know Elizabeth hadn't changed her will yet, and anyway she didn't set out to kill the old lady. She hoped to persuade her to let them move in with her, but Elizabeth wouldn't hear of it. 'A *baby* in the house,' she had said, 'at my age? I couldn't bear it, dear. I'm sorry.'

And that's when Mum lost it and pushed her mother downstairs. She's not a killer. She flipped, that's all. She's always been a super mum to me and it was the happiest day of my life when she finally came home.

I never told her I'm *her* mum, by the way. I never told anybody except Molly. Me and Molly had a talk, and she said it might be wise to hang on to *that* particular secret. She's OK, old Molly, in spite of what Auntie Anne says. I know Mum wonders how I knew about Grandma Elizabeth and Grandad Bob and the Glory Hole and all that and so does Dad, but when they ask I mumble about dreams and visions. They probably think I'm crazy but I don't mind.

The dream's gone, by the way. My nightmare. I don't get it any more and you can bet I don't miss it. I like to think it's because Grandma Elizabeth's happy now but whatever the reason, it's restful. Yeah, that's the word. Restful.

Oh – you might be wondering why Molly showed up in the allotments that night in the nick of time, like Superman rescuing Lois Lane. I'd have wondered myself if I hadn't been so screwed up. I asked her a long time after, and she told me she'd worried and worried over the dream I mentioned – the one where I was walking in a lonely spot. She knew my dreams had a way of coming true and that evening, sitting at home imagining me setting off for the Hallowe'en Rave, she'd remembered the short cut through the allotments from when *she* was at school, and everything clicked into place. It was an amazing example of intuition, and it must've cost her a terrific effort to get herself across town in her condition, but I wouldn't half have been pleased to see her if my auntie *had* been bent on murder.

Anything else? Oh, yes. Kylie Bickerdyke won the software. Well – I never got there, did I? Anyway, her triumph was short-lived because Pizza-face and some of her cronies waylaid her in the toilets and chucked her in the pond. She floated too, apparently, which proves she actually *is* a witch.

Funny old world, isn't it?

ROOM 13

Room 13 was inspired by a real school trip to Whitby by Year Two, from Mandale Middle School in Bradford, 1987.

To:

Robert Bates
Edward Benson
James Bentham
Andrea Boyes
Simon Carney
Clair Feltwell
Mark Hall
Craig Hobson
Elizabeth Holland
Louise Horsley
Andrew Howard
David Jenkinson
Samantha Lee
Gavin Ridealgh
John Robinson
Rachael Rowley
Amanda Whiteley
Victoria Winterburn

Who were there too.

I

This is what Fliss dreamed the night before the second year went to Whitby.

She was walking on a road high above the sea. It was dark. She was alone. Waves were breaking at the foot of cliffs to her left, and further out, the moonlight made a silver path on the water.

In front of her was a house. It was a tall house, looming blackly against the sky. There were many windows, all of them dark.

Fliss was afraid. She didn't want to go inside the house. She didn't even want to walk past but she had no control over her feet. They seemed to go by themselves, forcing her on.

She came to a gate. It was made of iron, worked into curly patterns. Near the top was a bit that was supposed to be a bird in flight – a seagull perhaps – but the gate had been painted black, and the paint had run and hardened into little stalactites along the bird's wings, making it look like a bat.

9

The gate opened by itself, and as she went through Fliss heard a voice that whispered, 'The Gate of Fate.' She was drawn along a short pathway and up some stone steps to the front door, which also opened by itself. 'The Keep of Sleep,' whispered the voice.

The door closed silently behind her. Moonlight shone coldly through a stained-glass panel into a gloomy hallway. At the far end were stairs that went up into blackness. She didn't want to climb that stairway but her feet drew her along the hallway and up.

She came to a landing with doors. The stairs took a turn and went on up. As Fliss climbed, it grew colder. There was another landing, more doors and another turn in the stair. Upward to a third landing, then a fourth, and then there were no more stairs. She was at the top of the house. There were four doors, each with a number. 10. 11. 12. 13. As she read the numbers, door thirteen swung inward with a squeal. 'No!' she whispered, but it was no use. Her feet carried her over the threshold and the voice hissed, 'The Room of Doom.'

In the room was a table. On the table stood a long, pale box. Fliss thought she knew what it was. It filled her with horror, and she whimpered helplessly as her feet drew her towards it. When she was close she saw a shape in the box and there was a smell like damp earth. When she was very close the voice whispered, 'The Bed of Dread,' and then the shape sat up and reached out for her and she screamed. Her screams woke her and she lay damp and trembling in her bed.

Her mother came and switched on the light and looked down at her. 'What is it, Felicity? I thought I heard you scream.'

Fliss nodded. 'I had a dream, Mum. A nightmare.'

'Poor Fliss.' Her mother sat down on the bed and stroked her hair. 'It's all the excitement, I expect – thinking about going away tomorrow.' She smiled. 'Try to go back to sleep, dear. You've a long day ahead of you.'

Fliss clutched her mother's arm. 'I don't want to go, Mum.'

'What?'

'I don't want to go. I want to drop out of the trip.'

'But why – not just because of a silly dream, surely?'

'Well, yes, I suppose so, Mum. It was about Whitby, I think. A house by the sea.'

'A house?'

'Yes.' She shivered, remembering. 'I was in this house and something horrible was after me. Can I drop out, Mum?'

Her mother sighed. 'I suppose you could, Felicity, if you're as upset as all that. I could ring Mrs Evans first thing, tell her not to expect you, but you might feel differently in the morning.' She smiled. 'Daylight makes us forget our dreams, or else they seem funny – even the scary ones. Let's decide in the morning, eh?'

Fliss smiled wanly. 'OK.' She knew she wouldn't forget her dream, and that it would never seem funny. But it was all right. She was in control of her feet (she wiggled them under the covers to make sure), and they weren't going to take her anywhere she didn't want to go.

If you were a second year there was a different feel about arriving at school that morning. Your friends were standing around in groups by the gate with bags and cases and no uniform, watching the other kids trail down the drive to begin another week of lessons.

You'd be going into school yourself, of course, but only for a few minutes. Only long enough to answer your name and listen to some final instructions from Mr Joyce. There was a coach at the bottom of the drive – a gleaming blue-and-white coach with tinted windows and brilliant chrome, waiting to whisk you beyond the reach of chairs and tables and bells and blackboards and all the sights and sounds and smells of school, to freedom, adventure and the sea. A week. A whole week, tingling with possibilities and bright with promise.

Fliss had changed her mind. Waking to the sun

in her window and birds in the garden, she had thought about her friends, and the sea, and the things which were waiting there, and her dream of the night before had seemed misty and unreal, which of course it was. Her mother had been pleased, and had resisted the temptation to say 'I told you so.'

She'd managed to persuade her parents not to come and see her off. Some parents always did, even when their kids were just off on a day trip. Fliss thought it was daft. Talking in loud voices so everyone could hear, saying stuff like 'Wrap up warm and stay away from the water and don't forget to phone so we'll know you arrived in one piece.' Plonkers.

Lisa Watmough was among the crowd by the gate. She was wearing jeans and talking to a girl called Ellie-May Sunderland. Fliss didn't like Ellie-May much. Nobody did. She was sulky, spoilt and selfish. But never mind. They were off to the seaside, weren't they? Fliss joined them, putting her suitcase on the ground next to Lisa's. 'Hi, you two. Nice morning.'

'Yeah.' They smiled at the sky. 'I can't wait to get on that beach,' said Fliss.

'I can't wait to see the hotel,' said Lisa. 'Mr Hepworth says it's called The Crow's Nest. I hope we're in the same room, Fliss.'

14

'You won't be,' said Ellie-May. 'Our Shelley went last year and she says Mrs Evans splits you up from your friends so you don't play about at night.'

'She might not this year. It's a different hotel. And anyway, me and Fliss wouldn't play about, would we, Fliss?'

Fliss shook her head and Ellie-May sniggered. 'Try telling Mrs Evans that.'

Lisa looked at her watch. It was nearly ten to nine. 'We'd better move,' she said. 'The sooner we get the boring bit over, the sooner we'll be off.' They picked up their luggage and set off down the drive.

Mr Hepworth was standing by the coach. As the girls approached he called out, 'Come on you three – hurry up. Leave your cases by the back of the bus and go into the hall.' The driver was stowing luggage in the boot, watched by a knot of parents. The three girls deposited their cases and hurried into school.

All the second-year kids were lined up in the hall, waiting for Mr Joyce. As Fliss got into line she felt somebody's breath on her cheek and a voice whispered the word 'Dracula' in her ear. She turned round to find Gary Bazzard grinning at her. She scowled. 'What you on about?'

'I said Dracula.'

15

'I know that, you div – what about him?'

'Lives in Whitby, doesn't he?'

'Does he naff! He's dead for a start, and when he was alive he lived in Transylvania.'

'No.' The boy shook his shaggy head. 'Whitby. Old Hepworth told us. And he's not dead neither. He's undead. He sleeps in a coffin in the daytime and goes out at night.'

Fliss felt a flicker of unease as the boy's words recalled her dream, but the headmaster appeared at that moment and began to address the assembly. He spoke of rambles, ruins and rock-pools as the sun streamed in through high windows and anticipation shone in the eyes of his listeners, but Fliss gazed at the floor, her lip caught between her teeth.

They were off by twenty-five past nine, growling slowly up the drive while Mr Joyce and a handful of parents stood in a haze of exhaust, waving.

Fliss and Lisa managed to get seats together. Lisa had the one by the window. As the coach turned on to the road she twisted round for a last glimpse of the school. 'Goodbye, Bottomtop!' she cried. 'And good riddance.'

'That'll do, Lisa Watmough.'

Startled, she turned. Mrs Evans was sitting two rows behind, glaring at her through the space between headrests.

'Yes, Miss.' She faced the front, dug Fliss in the ribs and giggled. 'I didn't know she was sitting so close. Where's Mrs Marriott?'

'Back seat, so she can keep an eye on us all. And Mr Hepworth's up there with the driver.'

'Huh! Trust teachers to grab all the best seats. Who's this in front of us?' The tops of two heads showed above the headrests.

'Gary Bazzard and David Trotter. I hope we're nowhere near them in the hotel.'

'You won't be,' said Ellie-May, who was sitting across the aisle from Fliss. 'Our Shelley says they put girls on one floor and boys on another so you don't see each other with nothing on.'

'Our Shelley,' sneered Fliss. 'Our Shelley says this, our Shelley says that. I hope we're not going to have a week of what our Shelley says, Ellie-May.'

'Huh!' Ellie-May tossed her head. 'I was telling you how it'll be, that's all, misery-guts. Anyway, you can naff off if you want to know owt else – you won't get it from me.'

'Good!' Fliss shuffled in her seat, turning as far from Ellie-May as she could, and sat scowling across Lisa at the passing scene.

Lisa looked at her. 'What's up with you?' she hissed. 'We're supposed to be enjoying ourselves and you look like somebody with toothache going into double maths.'

'It's her.' Fliss jerked her head in Ellie-May's direction. 'She gets on my nerves.'

'She was only telling you. You wanted to know if we'd be anywhere near Baz and Trot and she said we won't. What's wrong with that?'

Fliss shrugged. 'Nothing.'

'Well then.'

'I don't feel too good, right? I had this dream last night – a nightmare, and I couldn't sleep after it. And then this morning in the hall, Bazzard starts going on about Dracula. Saying he lives in Whitby, stuff like that, and I wasn't in the mood.'

Lisa pulled a face. 'No need to take it out on other people though, is there? You could go to sleep here, on the coach. Look – the seat tips back. Lie back and shut your eyes. There's nothing to look at anyway, unless you like the middle of Leeds.'

So Fliss pressed the button on the armrest and tipped her seat back, but then the boy in the seat behind yelled out that she was crushing his knees and demanded that she return it to its upright position. When she refused, settling back and closing her eyes, the boy, Grant Cooper, began rhythmically kicking the back of the seat, like somebody beating on a drum. Fliss sighed but kept her eyes closed, saying nothing. As she had anticipated, Mrs Evans soon noticed what the boy was up to. A hand came snaking through the gap between the headrests and grabbed a fistful of his hair. 'Ow!' he yelped. Mrs Evans rose, so that the top part of her face appeared over the seat. She began speaking very quietly to Grant Cooper, punctuating her words by alternately tightening and relaxing her grip on his hair.

'Grant Cooper.' (Squeeze) 'The upholstery on that seat cost a lot of money.' (Squeeze) 'It was fitted to make this coach both smart and comfortable.' (Squeeze) 'It was not provided so that horrible little so-and-sos like you could use it for football practice.' (Squeeze) 'How d'you think your mother would like it if somebody came into your house and started kicking the back of her three-piece suite, eh?' (Squeeze) 'Eh?' (Squeeze) 'Like it, would she?' (Squeeze)

'Please, Miss, no, Miss.' Grant's eyes were watering copiously and his mouth was twisted into a grimace which would not have been out of place in a medieval torture-chamber.

'Well, then,' (Squeeze) 'kindly show the same respect for other people's property that your mother would expect to be shown to hers. All right, Grant Cooper?' (Squeeze)

'Yes, Miss.' The grip loosened. The hand withdrew. Grant slumped, like a man cut down from the whipping-post, and wiped his eyes with the back of his hand. Mrs Evans' face sank from view. Fliss smiled faintly to herself, and drifted off to sleep.

4

Fliss opened her eyes as the coach swung into a tight turn which nearly catapulted her into the aisle. 'What's happening – where are we?'

'Pickering,' said Lisa. 'We're stopping. You've been asleep ages.'

Fliss looked out. They were rolling on to a big car-park with a wall round it. As the coach stopped, Mr Hepworth stood up at the front. 'This is Pickering,' he said. 'And we are making a toilet stop.' His eyes swept along the coach and locked on to those of a boy near the back. 'A toilet stop, Keith Halliday. Not a shopping stop. Not a sightseeing stop. Not a "let's buy packets of greasy fish and chips, scoff the lot before Sir sees us and then throw up all over the coach" stop. Have I made myself quite clear?'

'Sir.'

'Right. The toilets,' he pointed, 'are down there at the bottom of this car-park. To get into them,

21

you have to go out on to the pavement. It's a very busy road, and I don't want to see anyone trying to cross it. Neither do I want to see boys going into the ladies' toilet, or girls into the gents'. Have I said something funny, Andrew Roberts?'

'No, Sir.'

'Right.' He looked at his watch. 'It's ten past eleven. The coach will leave here at twenty-five past on the dot. Make sure you're on it, because it's a long walk back to Bradford.'

'When we get back on,' whispered Fliss to Lisa, 'it's my turn for the window seat, right?'

Lisa nodded. 'You feeling better, then?'

'Yes, thanks. I had a lovely sleep.'

'I know. You missed a lot, though. There was this field – a sloping field with millions of poppies in it. The whole field was red. It was ace.'

When Fliss got back on the coach there was no sign of Lisa. She sat down and watched the kids straggling across the tarmac in the warm sunshine. Soon, everybody was back on board except her friend. The driver had started the engine and Mrs Marriott was counting heads when Lisa appeared from behind the toilet block and came hurrying to the coach. As she clambered aboard, Mr Hepworth looked at his watch. 'What time did I say we'd be leaving, Lisa Watmough?'

Some of the children were sniggering and Lisa

blushed. 'Twenty-five past, Sir. I forgot the time, Sir.'

'You forgot the time. Well, for your information it is now twenty-six minutes to twelve, and we'll be lucky if we arrive at the hotel by midday, which is when we are expected. The meal which is being prepared for us might well be ruined, and it will be all your fault, Lisa Watmough.' He bent forward suddenly, peering at her jeans. 'What have you got there?' Something was making a bulge in the pocket of Lisa's jeans and she was trying to conceal it with her hand.

'Nothing, Sir.'

'Take it out and give it to me.'

'It's just this, Sir.' She pulled out an object wrapped in tissue paper and handed it over. The teacher stripped away the wrapping to reveal a green plastic torch in the shape of a dragon. The bulb and its protective glass were in the dragon's gaping mouth. Mr Hepworth held up the torch, using only his thumb and forefinger, and looked at it with an expression of extreme distaste.

'Did you bring this – this thing with you from home, Lisa Watmough?'

'No, Sir.'

'Oh. Then I suppose there's a little kiosk inside the ladies' toilet where patrons can do a bit of shopping. Am I right?'

23

'No, Sir.'

The teacher frowned. 'Then I'm afraid I don't understand. You didn't bring it from home, and you didn't get it in the ladies'. You haven't been anywhere else, yet here it is. Perhaps you laid it, like a hen lays an egg. Did you?'

'No, Sir.'

'Then what did you do?'

'I went in a shop, Sir.'

'You did what?'

'Went in a shop, Sir.'

'And what had I said about shopping, Lisa Watmough, just before you got off the coach?'

'We weren't to do any, Sir.'

'Right. Then why did you go into that shop?'

'I don't know, Sir.'

'You don't know, and neither do I, but here's something I do know. This evening, when the rest of the group is listening to a story in the hotel lounge, you will be in your room writing two apologies – one to the children for having kept them waiting, and one to me for having disobeyed my instructions. When both apologies have been written to my satisfaction, this torch will be returned to you. In the meantime you can leave it with me. Go to your seat.'

'What the heck did you do that for?' whispered Fliss, as Lisa slid into her seat. Lisa was one of those girls who seldom step out of line and are rarely in trouble at school.

She shook her head miserably. 'I don't know, Fliss. I don't even need a torch – I've got a better one at home. You'll think I'm crazy, but I couldn't help it – it was as though my feet were going by themselves.'

'Oh, don't you start,' groaned Fliss.

'What d'you mean?'

'Nothing. Forget it.' She looked out of the window. They passed a sign. North Yorkshire Moors National Park. The coach was climbing. Fliss gazed out as green pasture gave way to tree-less desolation. She shivered.

25

'Hey look!'

A boy on the right-hand side near the front of the coach stood up and pointed. Everybody looked. Out of the bleak landscape rose three white, dome-shaped objects, like gigantic mushrooms breaking through the earth. As the coach carried them closer, they saw a scatter of low buildings and a fence. The great spheres, gleaming in the sunlight, looked like objects in a science-fiction movie.

'Wow! What are they, Sir?'

Mr Hepworth got up. 'That's the Fylingdales early-warning station,' he told them. 'Inside those domes is radar equipment, operated by the British and American forces. It maintains a round-the-clock watch for incoming missiles. They say it would give us a three-minute warning.' He smiled wryly. 'Three minutes in which to do whatever we haven't done yet and always wanted to.'

'What would you do, Sir?' asked a grinning Waseem Kader.

'What would I do?' The teacher thought for a moment. 'I think I'd get a brick and throw it through the biggest window I could find.' He smiled. 'I've always fancied that.'

'Oh, I wouldn't, Sir – I'd run to the Chinese and get chicken chop-suey ten times and gobble it right quick.'

'Yeah!' cried Sarah-Jane Potts. 'That's what I'd do and all – we wouldn't have to pay, would we, Sir?'

'I'd get a big club and smash our Shelley's head in,' said Ellie-May. 'I hate her.'

'There'd be no point, fathead!' sneered a boy behind her. 'She'd be dead in three minutes anyway.'

The noise level rose. Excited voices called back and forth across the coach as everybody tried to outdo everybody else in what they'd do with their last three minutes. The fact that many of them would have needed several hours or even days to carry out their plans was disregarded, and the discussion continued till the vehicle topped the highest rise and Mrs Marriott raised her voice, drawing everybody's attention to the ruins of Whitby Abbey, which were now visible in the hazy distance.

Gary Bazzard knelt, leering at Fliss over the back of his seat. 'See – that's where Dracula lives – in the ruins. Old Hepworth told us.'

'Old Hepworth told you no such thing.'

The boy's remark had coincided with a lull in conversation as everybody strained for a glimpse of the abbey, and Mr Hepworth had heard it. 'Old Hepworth told you that Bram Stoker, who created the character of Dracula, was inspired to do so after having seen the ruined abbey. Dracula does not live there or anywhere else. He is a figment of Stoker's imagination, Gary Bazzard, and sometimes I wish the same might be said of you.'

There was laughter at this. The boy's cheeks reddened as he resumed his seat. Fliss smiled faintly, gazing out at the distant ruins and beyond them to the sea.

It was ten past twelve when the coach drew up outside The Crow's Nest Hotel. Mr and Mrs Wilkinson, who ran it, were standing on the top step waiting for them. Lisa flushed, remembering what Mr Hepworth had said about it being all her fault. She hoped he wouldn't point her out to the Wilkinsons as the culprit.

'Check under your seats and on the luggage rack,' warned Mrs Marriott, as everybody stood up. 'Don't leave any of your property in the coach.' The children checked, then filed slowly along the

28

aisle and down on to the pavement. It was sunny, but a breeze blew from the sea, making it cooler than it would now be in Bradford. The driver went round the back and started unloading bags and cases, which their owners quickly claimed.

Fliss looked at the hotel. There was something vaguely familiar about the steps. The porch. Even the breeze, and the distant sound of the sea.

When everybody had their luggage Mr Hepworth led them into the hotel. Fliss looked at the iron bird on the black gate. For a moment she thought it was meant to be a gull, but then she remembered the name of the place and decided it was probably a crow. Somebody had made a poor job of painting it. Drips had run down to the edges of its wings and hardened there, giving them a webbed, spiky appearance, so that it looked more like a bat than a bird.

'Right, listen!'

Lunch over, they had crammed themselves into the lounge with all their baggage, squeezing into chairs and settees, perching on the edges of tables, sitting on bags and cases on the floor while the three teachers sorted out room allocations and other matters with the Wilkinsons in the hall-way. They had taken in the view from the bay window, looked at the prints round the walls and were starting to get restless when Mr Hepworth stuck his head through the doorway.

'I'm waiting, Andrew Roberts.' The noise faded as Andrew Roberts stopped using the top of his suitcase as a drum and everybody looked towards the teacher. 'There are bedrooms on four floors in this hotel, and two rooms to a floor. I'm going to give you your room numbers now, and tell you which floor your room is on. As soon as you know your floor and number, I want you

30

to pick up your luggage and walk quietly up to
your room. What do I want you to do, Gemma
Carlisle?'

'Sir, go up to our room, Sir.'

'And how do I want you to go?'

'Walking quietly, Sir.'

'Right.' Mr Hepworth glared about the crowd-
ed room from under dark, bushy eyebrows.
'Walking quietly. Not charging up the stairs
like a crazed rhinoceros, swinging your case,
smashing vases and screaming at the top of
your voice. And when you find your room,
go in and wait. Don't touch anything, and
don't start fighting about whose bed is which,
or who's going to have this wardrobe or that
drawer. The teacher responsible for your floor
will come and sort all that out as soon as possible.' He put on his spectacles and began reading
from a list.

'Joanne O'Connor, Maureen O'Connor, Felicity Morgan and Marie Nero, top floor, room
ten.'

'Aw, Sir –'

'Moaning already, Felicity?'

'Me and Lisa wanted to be together, Sir.'

'Well you're not, are you? We'd be here all
day if we started trying to put everybody with
their best friend. Off you go.' He scanned his list

31

again. 'Vicky Holmes, Samantha Storey and Lisa Watmough, top floor, room eleven.'

Fliss carried her case up the stairs. There were brown photographs in frames all the way up. Ships and boats with sails. Old-time fisherfolk in bulky clothes. A wave breaking over a jetty.

Room ten contained a pair of bunk-beds and a double bed. There were two wardrobes, a chest of drawers and a dressing-table. The carpet was green and thin. A small washbasin stood in one corner. A brown photograph on the wall showed two children playing with a toy boat in a rock-pool.

Maureen went to the window. 'Hey! We're ever so high. You can see the sea from here.' Joanne and Marie went to look. Fliss put her case down and joined them. Beyond the road an expanse of close-mown grass, bisected by a footpath, stretched almost to the clifftop. There were wooden seats at intervals along the footpath. Away to the left was something which might be a crazy-golf course, while to the right stood a shelter with benches and large windows, and a telephone kiosk. In the shelter an old woman sat. She was dressed in black, and seemed to be looking straight at them. Beyond all this, glinting blue-grey under the sun, lay the sea.

'Isn't it lovely?' breathed Marie.

'Hmm.' Maureen's eyes followed a gull that swooped and soared along the line of the cliff. Joanne peered towards the horizon and thought she could make out the long, low shape of a ship – a tanker, perhaps.

Fliss gazed out to sea too, but she wasn't looking for a ship. She was thinking, Marie's right. It is lovely, but not nearly so beautiful as at night, when the moon makes a silver path across the water.

Behind them somebody knocked loudly on the door and flung it open. 'Hey, Fliss!' It was Lisa. 'We're right next door – come and see our room.'

Fliss was starting towards the door when Mrs Marriott's voice sounded on the landing. 'What are you doing there, Lisa Watmough? Didn't you hear Mr Hepworth say you were to wait in your room?'

'Yes, Miss.' There was a scampering noise. Lisa's face disappeared. Fliss waited a moment then looked out. There was nobody on the landing. The door of number eleven was half-open, and she heard Mrs Marriott asking Lisa if she didn't think she'd caused enough trouble for one day.

There were two other doors. One had twelve on it, and Fliss guessed that was the bathroom. The other had no number, but she knew what number it would have if it had. She was gazing at it, wondering what sort of room it concealed when Mrs Marriott came out of number eleven.

'Why are you standing there, Felicity Morgan?' she enquired.

'Please, Miss, I was just wondering what sort of room that is.' She pointed to the numberless door.

The teacher glanced at it. 'Linen cupboard, I should think.'

'It's big for a cupboard, Miss.'

The teacher nodded. 'Hotels need big cupboards, Felicity. All those sheets. Or it could be a broom cupboard, I suppose. Anyway, let's get your room organized.'

Felicity got the bottom bunk. She was glad. She hadn't fancied sharing the double bed. Mrs Marriott put Joanne and Maureen in that. They were twins, so that was all right. Marie had the top bunk. They had half an hour to unpack, put their things away and tidy up, then everybody was going down to the seafront for a look around.

Excited, anxious to be off, Fliss's three companions worked quickly. They chattered and giggled, but Fliss was silent. She was wondering when it was that she'd seen the sea under the moon, and noticing how broom rhymes with room, and also with doom.

7

It was three o'clock when the children gathered on the pavement outside the hotel. There were thirty-one of them, and Mr Hepworth split them into two groups of ten and one of eleven, with girls and boys in each group. 'Remember your group,' he said, 'because we'll be in groups a lot of the time while we're here.' Fliss found herself in Mrs Evans' group, and to her disgust Gary Bazzard was in it too. Gary was pretty disgusted himself, because his best friend David Trotter had ended up in Mrs Marriott's group. Lisa was in that group too.

It was breezy, but sunny and quite warm. The groups set off at intervals, turning right and walking in twos down North Terrace towards Captain Cook's monument and the whalebone arch. Fliss's group went second. As they passed the shelter, Fliss saw that the old woman was still there. She was gazing towards the hotel and seemed to be talking to herself. The first group was looking at the monument, so Mrs Evans led them to the arch.

'Now: can anybody tell me why there should be a whalebone arch at Whitby?' she asked. 'Yes, Roger?'

'For people to walk through, Miss.'

'Yes, Roger, I know it's for people to walk through, but why should it be made from whale-bone? Anybody?'

Tara Matejak raised her hand. She was Fliss's partner. 'Miss, because there were whaling ships at Whitby in the olden days.'

'That's right, Tara. And who knows why whales were valuable? Roger?'

'Oil, Miss. They used whale-oil for margarine and lamps and that. And they used the bones for women's dresses, Miss.'

'That's right.' Mrs Evans shielded her eyes with her hand and squinted up at the arch. 'What part of the whale's skeleton is this arch made from, d'you think?'

'Its jawbones, Miss,' said Maureen.

'Right. And they've put something on top, haven't they – it looks like an arrow. Can anybody guess what it actually is?'

Everybody gazed up at the object but nobody answered. After a moment Mrs Evans said, 'Well,

I'm not absolutely sure, but it looks to me like the tip of a harpoon. An old-fashioned harpoon – the sort they threw by hand from the bows of a whaleboat. Who's read *Moby Dick*?'

'Miss, I've seen *Jaws* on the telly.'

'What on earth has that got to do with it, Richard Varley?'

'Miss, nothing, Miss.'

'Then don't be so stupid, you silly boy!'

Nobody had read *Moby Dick*.

Mr Hepworth's group was now approaching, so Mrs Evans led Fliss and the others to Captain Cook's monument. They surrounded it, looking at the lengthy inscriptions on its plinth.

'Who can tell us something about Captain Cook?'

'Miss, he had one eye and one arm.'

'Rubbish, Michael Tostevin! That was Lord Nelson. Yes, Joanne?'

'He had a peg leg, Miss, and a parrot on his shoulder.'

'That was Long John Silver, dear – a fictitious character.' Mrs Evans sounded tired.

When they'd finished with Captain Cook, they went down a flight of stone steps on to a road called the Khyber Pass, and from there to the seafront. There, Mrs Evans turned them loose for a while to join their classmates on the sands, while she sank on to a bench which already supported her two colleagues.

Fliss found Lisa at the water's edge. 'What d'you think of it so far?'

Lisa pulled a face. 'Dead captains. Dead whales. Dead boring.'

Fliss laughed. 'It's OK down here though, isn't it?'

Lisa nodded. 'You bet. Let's find some flat pebbles and play at skimming.'

8

They played on the sand for an hour or so, until Mr Hepworth called them together at the foot of the slipway which connected the promenade with the beach.

'Right. What I thought we'd do between now and teatime is this: walk along the road here and have a look at the fish quay, then along the quay-side to the swing-bridge and over into the old town. There are lots of interesting shops in the old town, including some specializing in Whitby jet. We could have a look in some of the windows, but I don't think we should shop today – other-wise some of us might run out of pocket-money halfway through the week. At the end of the old town is a flight of steps leading up to the abbey and a church. There are a lot of steps, and I want you to count them as we go up and tell me how many there are. We'll go in groups again – d'you know your group, Barry Tune?'

'Sir.'

'Good. Here we go, then.'

The three teachers moved apart and called their groups to them. The children got into twos, and this time Fliss had Gary for a partner. He grinned at her. 'Holding hands, are we?'

'No chance. I've to eat my tea with this hand when we get back.'

'I'll be using a knife and fork.'

'Ha, ha, ha.'

They looked at the fish dock, but there were no boats in and the sheds with their stacks of fish-boxes were shut. They went along the quayside, threading their way between strolling holiday-makers, looking in shop windows or at the different kinds of boats in the harbour. There was that exciting smell in the air which you get at the seaside – that blend of salt and mud and fish and sweet rottenness which has you breathing deeply and makes you tingle.

They were taking their time – the evening meal was not until six-thirty – and Fliss was looking at a coble with her name, *Felicity*, painted on its prow when Gary grabbed her hand and cried, 'Hey – look at this!'

'What?' She spoke irritably and jerked her hand away, but looked where he pointed and saw a narrow building with dark windows and a sign which said 'The Dracula Experience'. A tall man with a pale face, dressed all in black, smiled from the doorway at the passing group. His teeth seemed quite ordinary.

Gary raised his hand and waved it at Mrs Evans. 'Miss – can we go in here, Miss, please?'

Mrs Evans, who had been looking out over the harbour, turned. She saw the building, read the sign, smiled faintly and shook her head. 'Not just now, Gary. On Thursday, everybody will be given some free time to shop for presents and spend what's left of their money in whatever way they choose. You'll be able to buy yourself some Dracula Experience then.' She looked into the eyes of the smiling man and added, loudly, 'If you must.'

They crossed the bridge and sauntered through the narrow streets of the old town till they came to the church steps. By the time they reached the top, Fliss was out of breath. She'd counted a hundred and ninety-seven steps but Mr Hepworth, whose group had got there first, said there were a hundred and ninety-nine and she believed him.

The top of the steps gave on to an old graveyard. Weathered stones leaned at various angles, so eroded you couldn't read the epitaphs. Long grass rippled in the wind. There was a church, and a breathtaking view of Whitby and the sea.

They had a look inside the church. It was called St Mary's. Mr Hepworth pointed out its special features. You could buy postcards and souvenirs by the door. Fliss bought a postcard of the ruined abbey to send home. When they were gathered outside she said, 'Are we going to the ruins, Sir?' She wasn't sure whether she wanted to or not.

'Not today, Felicity. We'll be looking at them on Wednesday morning, before we set off to walk to Saltwick Bay.'

They poked about in the churchyard for a while and visited the toilets near the abbey. Then they descended the hundred and ninety-nine steps and began making their way back to The Crow's Nest. The fresh air and exercise had sharpened everybody's appetite, and most of the children spent the walk back wondering what was for tea. Fliss did not. She was thinking about the landing at the top of the house, and what it would be like in the dark. The funny thing was, she seemed to know.

9

They got back in plenty of time for tea, which was eggs, chips and sausages, with swiss-roll and ice-cream for pudding. Afterwards everybody went upstairs to put on tracksuits and trainers. Mrs Marriott was taking them for a game of rounders on the sands. Lisa would be missing out, because of the apologies she had to write.

Gary Bazzard's room was one floor below Fliss's. Number seven. When she came down the stairs he was standing in the doorway showing something to a group of his friends, who were making admiring noises. As Fliss passed he called out, 'How about this, Fliss?'

She glanced in his direction. He was holding up the biggest stick of rock she'd ever seen. She didn't like him much, and would have loved to walk on with her nose in the air, but the pink stick really was enormous: nearly a metre long and about four centimetres thick. She stopped. 'Where the heck did you get that from?' she asked, in what she hoped was a scornful voice.

'Shop on the quay. One pound fifty. No one saw me 'cause I stuck it down my jeans' leg.' His friends gasped and chuckled at his daring.

Fliss pulled a face. 'You're nuts. One pound fifty? I wouldn't give you fifty pence for it.'

'You wouldn't get chance.'

'It'll rot your teeth, so there.'

'You're only jealous.'

'I'm not. I hope Mr Hepworth catches you and hits you on the head with it.'

It was a good game of rounders. It was more fun than it might have been, because the tide was coming in and the strip of sand they were playing on grew narrower and narrower. People kept hitting the ball into the sea, and some of the fielders had to play barefoot so that they could retrieve it. Finally the pitch became so restricted that play was impossible. They wrapped up the game, retreated to the top of one of the concrete buttresses which protected the foot of the cliff and sat, watching the tide come in.

Cocoa and biscuits were served in the lounge at half-past eight. The children sat sipping and munching while twilight fell outside and Mrs Evans read them a story. Lisa came down with her written apologies. Mr Hepworth read them, nodded, and gave her back her torch. It was nine o'clock. Bedtime.

Fliss was tired, but she couldn't sleep. It was fun at first, lying in the dark, talking with Marie and the twins, but one by one they drifted off to sleep and she was left listening to the muffled noises that rose from the boys' room below. After a while these too stopped, and then there was only the occasional creak, and the rhythmic shush of the sea.

She lay staring at the ceiling, waiting for her eyes to get tired. If the lids grew heavy enough they'd close, and then she'd drift off. She wouldn't even know she was lying in the dark, and when she woke up it would be morning and the first night – the worst night – would be over.

Phantom lights swam across her field of vision, lazily, like shoals of tiny fish. She watched them, but they failed to lull her, and presently it came to her that she would have to go to the bathroom.

She listened. If somebody else was awake somewhere it would be easier. A boy on the floor below perhaps, or one of the teachers. She looked at her watch. 23.56. Four minutes to midnight. Surely somebody was still about – the Wilkinsons, locking up for the night, or Mr Hepworth making a final patrol.

Silence. In all the world, only Fliss was awake.

She listened to the steady breathing of the other three girls. Why couldn't one of them have been a snorer? If somebody had been snoring she could have given them a shake. A policeman going by outside would be better than nothing – his footsteps might make her feel safe. But there was no policeman. There wasn't even a car.

The bed creaked as she sat up and swung her legs out. She listened. Nothing. The steady breathing continued. She hadn't disturbed anybody. Perhaps she'd have to put the light on to find the door – that would wake them. But no. There was moonlight and the curtains were thin and she could see quite clearly. It would be most unfair to wake them with the light.

She stood up and crept towards the door. There was sand in the carpet. A floorboard creaked and she paused, hopefully. One of the twins stirred, mumbling, and Fliss whispered, 'Maureen? Joanne?' but there was no response.

She opened the door a crack and looked out. The only illumination came from a small window on the half-landing below. It was minimal. She could make out the dark shapes of the doors but not the pattern on the carpet. The air had a musty smell and felt cold.

As she hesitated for a moment in the doorway, peering into the gloom and listening, she became

46

aware of a faint sound – the snuffling, grunting noise of somebody snoring beyond the door of room eleven. She found it oddly reassuring, and crossed the landing quickly in case it should stop.

Re-crossing a minute later with the hiss of the toilet cistern in her ears, she could still hear it. It seemed louder, and was accompanied now by a thin, whimpering noise, like crying. Fliss pulled a face. Somebody feeling homesick. Not Lisa, surely?

The idea that her friend might be in distress made her forget her fear for a moment. She took a couple of steps towards room eleven, unsure of what she intended to do. As she did so, she became aware that the noise was not coming from that room at all, but from the one next to it – the cupboard. Her eyes flicked to its door. On it, visible in the midnight gloom, was the number thirteen.

She recoiled, covering her mouth with her hand. When she had asked Mrs Marriott what lay beyond that door, there had been no number on it. She knew there hadn't, yet there it was. Thirteen. And somebody was in there. Somebody, or some thing.

She backed away. The hissing of the cistern dwindled and ceased. The other sounds continued, and now the whimpering was more persistent, and the snuffling had a viscous quality to it, like a pig rooting in mud.

She retreated slowly, holding her breath. When she reached the doorway of her own room she backed through it, feeling for the doorknob and keeping her eyes fixed on the door of room thirteen. Once inside, she closed the door quickly, crossed to her bed and lay staring at the ceiling while spasms shook her body.

Much later, when the shivering had stopped and she was drifting to sleep, she thought she heard stealthy footsteps on the landing, but when she woke at seven with the sun in her face and her friends' excited chatter in her ears, she wondered whether she might have dreamed it all.

10

They gathered in the lounge after breakfast. Mr Hepworth had fixed a large map of the coast to the wall. He pointed. 'Here's Whitby, where we are. And here,' he slid his finger northward along the coastline, 'is Staithes, where the coach will drop us this morning. Staithes used to be an important fishing port like Whitby, and there are still a few fishermen there, but it is a quiet village now. Captain Cook worked in a shop at Staithes when he was very young – before he decided to be a sailor.'

'Will we be going in the shop, Sir?'

'No, Neil Atkinson, we will not. Unfortunately, it was washed away by the sea a long time ago. However, if we are very lucky we might see a ghost.'

There were gasps and exclamations at this. 'Captain Cook's ghost, Sir?' asked James Garside. The teacher shook his head, smiling. 'No, James.

49

Not Captain Cook's. A young girl's. There's a dangerous cliff at Staithes, a crumbling cliff, and the story goes that when this girl was walking under it one day, a chunk of rock fell and decapitated her. Who knows what decapitated means? Yes, Steven Jackson?'

'Sir, knocked her cap off, Sir.'

'No. Michelle Webster?'

'Squashed her, Sir?'

'Closer, but not right. 'Ellie-May Sunderland?'

'Sir, knocked her head off, Sir.'

'Correct.' He leaned forward, peering at the girl through narrowed eyes. 'Are you all right, Ellie-May – you look a bit pasty?'

'Yes, Sir.'

'Sure?'

'Yes, Sir.'

'Right. Well, there's a bridge over a creek at Staithes, and that's where the headless ghost has been seen. We'll be having a look round the village, then walking along the clifftop path to Runswick Bay. That's here.' He jabbed at the map again. A boy raised his hand.

'What is it, Robert Field?'

'How far is it, Sir?'

The teacher shrugged, smiling. 'A few miles. We'll find somewhere to eat our packed lunches on the way, and the coach will be waiting at

Runswick to bring us back here. Right – it's a lovely sunny morning, so let's get started.'

Lisa saved Fliss a seat on the coach. As they roared along the coast road she said, 'We stayed awake ever so late in our room last night, talking. Telling jokes and that. It was brilliant.'

'You were all asleep before midnight, though,' said Fliss.

'How d'you know?'

'I passed your door at midnight. There wasn't a sound.'

'What were you doing, passing our door at midnight?'

'I went to the toilet. Or at least I think I did.'

'How d'you mean, you think you did – don't you know?'

Fliss pulled a face. 'No. It's all mixed up with this horrible dream I had.'

'What was it about, your dream?'

Fliss told her friend about the strange noises that had seemed to come from the linen cupboard, the number thirteen on the door, the footsteps she thought she'd heard later. 'It all seemed so real, Lisa. But then this morning I looked, and of course there was no number on the door and the sun was shining and everybody was shouting and messing about on the landing, and it didn't seem real any more. D'you know what I mean?'

Lisa nodded. 'Sure. It was all a dream – you didn't go to the toilet and you weren't outside our door at midnight so you don't know what time we went to sleep, right?'

'Right. Except –'

'Except what, Fliss? What is it?'

'After the toilet, I dreamed I washed my hands, right? And it was one of those spurty taps where the water comes all at once and goes everywhere. Some went on the floor. Quite a lot, in fact. There didn't seem to be anything to mop it up with, and anyway I was too scared to hang about so I left it.'

Lisa shrugged. 'Dream water in a dream bathroom. So what?'

Fliss looked at her friend. 'It was still there this morning,' she said.

II

They spent an hour in Staithes, but nobody saw the ghost. They saw crab pots piled by cottage doors and boats tied up in the creek. They stared at the dangerous cliff and tried to imagine what it would be like to be walking along quite normally one second, and to have no head the next. They bought sweets and ice-lollies and stood among their knapsacks and shoulder-bags, chatting and watching the waves while the teachers had a cup of tea. At eleven o'clock they picked up their bags and moved out, leaving the village by way of a steep, winding footpath which led to the clifftop and on out of sight. Mr Hepworth said, 'This is part of the Cleveland Way, and it will take us to Runswick Bay. It's a three-mile walk, more or less. About halfway, we'll stop and eat our lunches. There's no tearing hurry, but do try to keep up – the path runs very close to the cliff edge in places, and if there are stragglers it becomes difficult to keep an eye on everybody. Are you listening, John Phelan?'

'Yessir.'

'Good. Off we go, then.'

The sun was a fuzzy ball above the sea. Little white clouds sailed inland on the breeze, their shadows racing across a rolling landscape of wheat field and meadow. Strung out in twos and threes along the track, the children walked and chattered. Gulls wheeled and soared, or floated like scraps of paper on the water far below. A jet, miles high, drew a thin white line across the sky.

Lisa flung out her arms and laughed. 'Lovely!' she cried. 'Don't you think it's lovely, Fliss – the smells? All this space?'

Fliss nodded. 'I was just thinking about the others, stuck in school having boring lessons, and us here enjoying ourselves.' She looked at her watch. 'We'd be in French now.'

'Did you have to mention that?' scowled Lisa. 'Trying to spoil my day, I know.'

'No, I'm not. I think it makes it better, thinking about where you'd be if you weren't here. It makes you appreciate it more.'

'Yeah, well, I can appreciate it without having to think about French, thank you very much. Are you still bothered about that dream, by the way?'

Fliss looked at her friend. 'Now who's trying to

spoil whose day?' She thought for a while. 'No, I'm not worried. Not at the moment. Not here. It's like I told you – in broad daylight all that sort of stuff seems daft. You say to yourself, it was just a dream, and you believe it. It's when you're in bed at night and everything's quiet that you start wondering. Anyway, I don't want to think about it now. What kind of bird's that?' She pointed. 'The black one with a grey head. I've seen a few of them today.'

Lisa shrugged. 'I don't know. I'm no good at birds. Ask Mrs Evans.'

Fliss looked behind. 'Where is Mrs Evans – I thought she was walking at the back?'

'She was. We must be going too fast for her or something. Either that or she's fallen off the cliff. Anyway, you could ask Mrs Marriott instead – she's just up there.'

Fliss giggled. 'You mean it doesn't matter if Mrs Evans has fallen into the sea, because she's not the only one who can identify birds?'

'No, you div – I never said that. Anyway, she won't have fallen, will she? We've left her behind, that's all. She hasn't kept up like old Hepworth said – I wonder if he'll make her write an apology?'

'Will he heck! D'you think we should tell somebody?'

'Can if you want. Mrs Marriott's just up there.'

Fliss put on a spurt, swerved past Helen Smith and Robert Field, and touched the teacher's shoulder.

'Miss.'

Mrs Marriott turned her head. 'What is it, Felicity?'

'We can't see Mrs Evans, Miss. She was at the back, and now she's disappeared. We thought we should mention it, Miss.'

'Hmm.' Mrs Marriott looked back over the quarter mile or so of track which was visible from where they were standing. Children passed them, leaving the path to do so. 'Thank you, Felicity. D'you think you could catch up with Mr Hepworth – tell him I sent you and ask him to stop the walk? She's probably just fallen behind, but I think perhaps we ought to wait for her.'

'Yes, Miss.'

She set off along the track, weaving in and out among her classmates. One or two called after her, demanding to know where she thought she was going or what the rush was about but she ignored them, going at a steady jog and keeping her eyes on Mr Hepworth.

She was still a couple of hundred metres behind him when he stopped and looked back. She waved and shouted, 'Sir – Sir!' and to her relief he raised his hand, halting the column, and stood watching her approach.

'What is it, Felicity?' he asked, as she came panting up to him. She told him and he shaded his eyes with his hand, peering back the way they'd come.

'Hmm. Well. She's nowhere in sight – probably twisted an ankle or something and fallen behind. We'll wait here a minute or two, and if she doesn't show up I'll go back and have a look.'

The line shortened, as those further back caught up and stopped. The children milled about, wondering what was happening, and a girl called out, 'Is this where we eat our lunch, Sir?'

Mr Hepworth shook his head. 'No, Samantha Varley, it is not. We're waiting for Mrs Evans, who has fallen behind a bit.' He said something quietly to Mrs Marriott, who came along the line counting heads.

'One missing,' she called. 'Is it Ellie-May? I don't think I've seen her.'

'It is, Miss,' said Haley Denton. 'I saw her dropping back, ages ago.'

'That's probably it, then,' said Mr Hepworth. 'Ellie-May fell behind and Mrs Evans is walking with her. I thought she wasn't looking too bright, back at the hotel.' He looked at his watch. 'We'll give them five minutes, then I'll set off back. Take your packs off and sit down – we might as well take a breather while we can.'

Fliss went back to sit with Lisa, but she hadn't been sitting for more than a minute when one of the boys yelled, 'They're coming, Sir!'

Everybody watched as the two figures approached. When they reached the place where Fliss and Lisa were sitting, Mrs Evans said, 'Now then, Ellie–May. You sit with Felicity and Lisa. They'll look after you.' She smiled, putting Ellie-May's knapsack, which she'd been carrying, on the grass. 'Ellie-May's not feeling very well, girls. You'll look after her, won't you?'

'Yes, Miss.'

'I knew you would.' She smiled again and moved on, murmuring, 'Sensible girls. Nice, sensible girls.'

Ellie-May looked awful. Her cheeks were white and there were dark smudges, like bruises, under her eyes. She sat down. 'I couldn't keep up,' she growled. 'I tried, but I went all dizzy. Silly Mrs Evans made me sit with my head between my knees for a bit and I had to drink tea from her flask. It tasted awful. As soon as I felt a bit better we set off after you at about fifty miles an hour, and now I feel rotten again.'

'Mrs Evans is nice,' said Lisa. 'She carried your pack, didn't she? What's the matter with you anyway – tummy bug or something?'

Ellie-May scowled. 'I don't know, do I, fat-head? Why do you ask such stupid questions?'

'Hey, Sunderland!' A group of boys was sitting nearby. One of them, David Trotter, grinned across at Ellie-May. 'If you didn't go creeping about in the middle of the night, we wouldn't have to hang around waiting for you when we're supposed to be out walking.'

Ellie-May shook her head. 'I don't know what you're talking about. I don't creep around. I was asleep all night.'

'Ooh, you lying so-and-so! I saw you. Half-past two, it was. You'd been to the top floor. You came down on to our landing and disappeared down the stairs. I was watching you from the bathroom.'

'No, you weren't, you spaz. You couldn't. I never left the room, so there!'

'Blue pyjamas with rabbits on, right?'

'Shut up. I don't know what you're on about.'

'I'm on about your pyjamas. You've got blue ones with rabbits on, haven't you?

'So what?'

'So how would I know that if I didn't see you?'

'I dunno. Maybe you were on the stairs or something when I was getting ready for bed. Maybe it's you that creeps about in the night.'

Fliss sat chewing on a grass stalk, gazing out to sea. She was thinking about last night. The noises from the cupboard. The footsteps. Lisa had said it was a dream and she'd tried to believe it was, but there was the water on the bathroom floor, and now this. She'd heard footsteps in the small hours, and Ellie-May had been seen coming down the stairs in pyjamas. Pyjamas with rabbits on them. So maybe it wasn't a dream, but if it wasn't a dream what was it? Had Ellie-May been in the cupboard last night? Was that possible? It was where the noises had come from, but then what about the number? If the noises were real so was the number, yet it wasn't there this morning. And anyway, why would anyone be in a cupboard at two in the morning? The whole thing was crazy. Unless –

She shivered.

12

'Right – this'll do nicely,' said Mr Hepworth. They'd reached a grassy hollow where the land ran down in a gentle slope to a cliff which was neither sheer nor high. The grass was very green and quite short, and the children sat down on it and took out their lunch-packs. Friends sat together, and the three teachers found a spot near the top of the slope from which they could see what everybody was doing.

Fliss grabbed Lisa's elbow and steered her away from the group she'd been about to join. 'I've got to talk to you,' she hissed. Ellie-May stood, wondering whether to go with them or stay with the group. Fliss turned and called, 'See you in a bit, Ellie-May – OK?'

Ellie-May nodded. 'Sure.' She sat down between Haley and Bobby Tuke. If people didn't want her around she wasn't going to worry about it.

'What's up?' said Lisa, when they'd got settled.

61

Fliss swallowed a mouthful of fishpaste sand-wich. 'You heard what Trotter said back there. About her?' She nodded towards Ellie-May, who was sitting with her back to them.

Lisa nodded. 'I think he made it up. He's like that.'

Fliss shook her head. 'I don't. I heard footsteps, didn't I? I think it was Ellie-May, and I think she was in that cupboard when I went to the bath-room.'

Her friend looked at her. 'Don't be silly, Fliss! It was a dream. Why would Ellie-May sit in a cup-board in the middle of the night, making funny noises? Why would anybody? And how could a door have a number on it at midnight, and none in the morning? You're barmy.'

'No, I'm not. What about the water on the bath-room floor?'

'Anybody could have squirted water on the floor. People do it on purpose, don't they?'

'Well, what about Ellie-May, then – what d'you think's wrong with her?'

Lisa shrugged. I dunno. I'm not a doctor, am I? Maybe she's got food-poisoning, which we all will after these rotten sandwiches.' She pulled a face, chewing. 'Why – what do you think's wrong, Doctor Morgan?'

'I think something happened to her in that

62

cupboard. I wasn't dreaming at all. I know that now. I'm off over to talk to Trot.'

She got up and went over to where David Trotter was sitting with a group of his friends. The boys stopped talking at her approach and squinted up at her, shielding their eyes with their hands. 'What do you want, mong-features?' asked Gary Bazzard, through a mouthful of something pink. Fliss ignored him. 'Can I have a word please, Trot?'

'Trot!' whooped Richard Varley. 'What is she, Trot – your girlfriend or something?'

Trotter blushed. 'Is she heck.' He scowled up at Fliss. 'What about?'

'I'll tell you over there.' She nodded towards a vacant spot on the slope. The others laughed. 'Watch her, Trot,' said Bazzard, 'she's after you.'

The red-faced boy scrambled to his feet. 'Come on then,' he growled. 'And it better be important or I'll chuck you off the cliff.'

They moved away from the others, and Fliss told him what she'd seen and heard in the night, linking it with what he'd seen and with Ellie-May's present condition. The boy glanced across at Ellie-May once or twice while she was speaking, and when she'd finished he nodded. 'OK. It all fits, and she looks rough, no doubt about that. But what I don't get is, why would she go up two floors and into a cupboard in the first place, and if she did, and something happened to her there – something bad – why hasn't she told one of the teachers?'

Fliss shrugged. 'I don't know, Trot, but there's something funny going on, isn't there?'

'Maybe. But what d'you want me to do about it?'

'I don't want you to do anything. Not by yourself. I'm thinking of keeping watch tonight to see if Ellie-May goes walkabout again. I think Lisa will join me. Will you?'

'I dunno. It seems daft to me. I mean, a cupboard. I ask you – what could there be in a cupboard, Felicity?'

'Fliss.'

'What?'

'Fliss. Call me Fliss.'

'Oh, I see. What could be in a cupboard, Fliss?'

'Who knows?' She chuckled. 'The point is, dare you keep watch with us and find out?'

'How d'you mean, dare I? D'you think I'm scared or something?'

'Could be.'

'Well, I'm not, I can tell you that.'

'Prove it. Watch with us.'

'OK, if Gary can come too.'

'How d'you know he wants to?'

'I don't, yet. He doesn't know anything about it, but he'll want to be in on it when he does. Can I tell him?'

Fliss sighed. 'I suppose so. But get him by himself, right? We don't want the whole flipping class stampeding around in the middle of the night, or nothing will happen at all.'

The boy smiled. 'I don't think it will anyway.'

'Well, we'll see, won't we?' said Fliss.

Somewhere between lunch and Runswick Bay, David must have filled his friend in on the events of the night before, and on Fliss's plan for that night. As he passed her seat on the coach, Gary bent down and whispered, 'OK – I'm in. Talk to you later.'

Clouds rolled in after tea, threatening rain. Team games on the beach were cancelled, and everybody went to their rooms to write up the day's activity. Each child was keeping a sort of log or diary of the visit, in which points of interest were to be recorded. Fliss wrote for a while, then got up and looked out of the window. The old woman was there watching the hotel. Fliss resolved to ask Mrs Wilkinson about her. She sat down again on her bunk, chewing the end of her pencil and reading through what she had written.

'Tuesday. Staithes and Runswick Bay. Nothing

happened on coach. Looked at scenery. Staithes old-fashioned and sort of dark with hills and cliffs all round. Mr Hepworth told us about the headless ghost but we didn't see it. We didn't see Captain Cook's shop either because it is under the sea. Crab pots everywhere. I had an ice-lolly and Mrs Marriott took our photo.'

'How d'you spell "excitement"?' asked Marie from her perch on the top bunk.

'Why – what're you writing about?'

'Mrs Evans. I'm putting, "There was a bit of excitement when we thought Mrs Evans had fallen off the cliff, but she'd only fallen behind, which was boring."'

'You're not.'

'I am.'

'I wouldn't be you, then. It's E-X-C-I-T-E-M-E-N-T.'

'Ta.'

Fliss knew she should write more, but she couldn't concentrate. If Lisa and the two boys were to watch with her tonight, they'd have to get together sometime this evening and sort out details, like where they'd meet and at what time.

She listened. Beyond the door, everything seemed quiet. Nobody was on the landing or the stairs. She wondered what the teachers were doing. If they were busy, she and Lisa might be able to slip down to the next floor and have a quick meeting with the boys. It was strictly forbidden to visit other people's rooms, but they'd have to risk it. She put her book and pencil on the bed and went to the door.

'Where you going?' asked Maureen.

'Toilet,' she lied, opening the door and looking out. The landing was deserted. She slipped out, closed the door and knocked on the door of room eleven.

'Who is it?' Samantha's voice.

'Fliss. Is Lisa there?'

'Yes. Just a minute.'

Voices beyond the door. Fliss glanced towards the cupboard. No number. Door eleven opened and Lisa looked out. 'Come on,' whispered Fliss.

'Where? I'm halfway through my log.'

'Trot's room. Make plans. Quiet.'

'OK.'

They tiptoed down the stairs, listening for teachers. There was nobody on the landing below. Doors seven and eight were closed.

'Which is theirs?' hissed Lisa.

'Seven. Watch the stairs while I knock.'

Lisa watched and listened. Fliss knocked.

'Who's there?' It sounded like Gary's voice.

'Fliss. Open up, quick.'

Footsteps approached the door. It opened a

crack. An eye peered out. 'On your own, are you?'

'Me and Lisa. Hurry up.'

The door opened. Gary and David came out. 'Aren't we using your room?' Fliss asked.

'No chance. Barry and Richard're in there. They know nothing about this. It'll have to be the bathroom.'

They slipped into the bathroom, and Gary pushed the door-catch into place. 'We'll have to make it quick,' he whispered. 'Somebody's bound to want the toilet before long, and anyway I haven't started my log yet.'

They made their plans swiftly. They would go to bed at nine as normal, and wait till their roommates fell asleep. That should be earlier than last night because they'd had a long, tiring walk. At twenty-five past eleven exactly they'd get out of bed. They wouldn't dress for fear of waking somebody. They would leave their rooms and meet in the top-floor bathroom, room twelve, at half-past eleven. From there they would be able to keep watch on the stair-top, landing and cupboard. It would be impossible for anyone to reach the cupboard without being seen, and if anything odd happened to the door itself, like the number thirteen suddenly appearing on it, they'd see that too.

This settled, the four split up and returned to their rooms. It wasn't until Fliss was lying in bed at half-past nine, listening to Marie and the twins, that she realized nobody had thought about what they'd do if Ellie-May did appear. She lay, worrying about this and looking at her watch every minute or two, as her room-mates chattered on.

It was nearly eleven o'clock before the girls in room ten stopped talking and three of them fell asleep. Fliss lay absolutely still, listening to their breathing, and almost drifted off herself. When she realized what was happening she shook her head, blinked rapidly and looked at her watch.

Twenty-three twenty. Ten minutes to zero. Now that it was nearly time she didn't fancy it one bit. The cold, dark landing. The door of the linen cupboard, upon which the number thirteen might at this very moment be materializing. The prospect of footfalls on the stair.

And I was the one who suggested it, she reminded herself. I must have been crazy.

Well, anyway, it was too late now. It was her plan and she was stuck with it. She squinted at her watch again. Twenty-three twenty-seven. Three minutes to zero. What she'd do was, she'd listen for the others arriving. One of the others, at least.

She didn't want to be the first. She knew that if she opened the door and found herself alone on the landing, just a metre or so from that creepy cupboard, she'd have the door shut and be back under the covers so quick her feet wouldn't touch the floor.

Listen. A creak somewhere. Somewhere a tick. The house, settling. Twenty-three twenty-nine, and no footsteps. Perhaps nobody'll turn up. Maybe they've fallen asleep. I nearly did. And if they have, it's off. There's no way I'm watching alone. No way. Please God, let them be asleep.

Zero hour, and listen – somebody's coming. Somebody's right outside the door, breathing. Waiting. And there – there goes a whisper, so there's two of them at least and they're whispering about me – asking where I am.

Asleep, that's where I am, so leave me. Let me sleep. There's three of you. You don't need me. You don't need me, do you? Do you?

Twenty-three thirty-one. Zero plus one. They're listening at the door, and they know you're not asleep. They can hear you breathing – looking at your watch. They can hear your heart.

My idea. My plan. My own stupid fault in other words. OK, OK. I'm coming. Here I come.

She got out of bed, tiptoed across the sandy carpet and stood with her ear to the door, listening to the sounds of stealthy movement beyond. Behind her, the three girls slept on. She twisted the knob and eased the door open. It squeaked, and somebody outside went, 'Sssh!' She looked across. Three pale figures were watching her from the bathroom doorway.

'Where the heck have you been?' hissed Lisa, as Fliss joined them. 'We've been here ages.'

'Sorry. I think I must have dropped off to sleep. Is anything happening?'

She looked towards the cupboard but there was no number. Trot shook his head. 'Nothing yet. Look, let's get inside and close the door except for a crack to look through. And no more talking, right?'

They stood on the cold plastic tiles, peering over one another's shoulders. The rain which had threatened earlier was now falling. Cloud hid the moon, so that the windows on the half-landings gave almost no light. Fliss shivered, wishing she had her dressing-gown and slippers, or better still, that she was where they were, in her bedroom at home.

Somewhere a clock chimed. 'What time's that?' whispered Gary. 'I forgot my flipping watch.'

Fliss looked at hers. 'Twenty-three forty-five – quarter to twelve.'

'Good grief, is that all? It feels like we've been

here for ever.' He withdrew from the doorway and walked up and down, hugging himself and shivering. Trot and Lisa drew back too, leaving Fliss to watch.

Nothing happened. After a while she said, 'Hey, how about somebody else taking a turn here? I need to get warm too.'

'I'll do it,' volunteered Lisa. Fliss went and stood on one leg beside the bath, resting a cold foot on its rim in order to massage some warmth into it. After a while she swapped over and rubbed the other foot.

Presently they heard the distant chimes again. Midnight. They looked at one another and drifted towards the door. As they did so, Lisa let out a stifled cry and pointed. 'Look.' They looked. The cupboard was room thirteen.

'Oh, wow,' moaned Gary. 'It's real. I thought it was a dream, but it's real.'

'You scared then?' Trot's words carried a challenge, but his voice came out a croak.

'I told you, didn't I?' breathed Fliss. 'I told you it wasn't a dream.'

'Oh, Fliss,' whimpered Lisa. 'Oh, my God, what am I doing here?' Fliss put an arm round her friend and squeezed. 'It's OK, Lisa. Take it easy. It's just a door with a number on it, right? We don't have to go in there or anything. We

don't even have to go near it, for goodness sake.'
She looked at the others. 'What now?'

'Listen!' Trot was watching the stairs. 'I think
someone's coming.'

'Oh, no!' Gary crammed all of his fingers in his
mouth and stood, gazing at the stair-top and shaking his head.

There came the unmistakable sound of footfalls
slowly ascending, and a pale shape came into view.
Trot grabbed Fliss's arm. 'It's Ellie-May.'

'Sssh!'

'But shouldn't we try to stop her? Look where
she's going for heaven's sake.'

'No!' Fliss shook her head. 'She's asleep, I think
– sleepwalking, and you're not supposed to wake
sleepwalkers. We'll watch what happens and tell
the teachers in the morning.'

Lisa looked at her. 'That was part of the plan,
was it?'

'Yes.' It wasn't, of course. She hadn't even considered what they might do if events reached this
stage. She only knew she couldn't leave this bathroom right now to save her life. Hers, or anybody
else's.

They watched. Ellie-May crossed the landing to
the cupboard door and reached for the knob. She
hesitated for a moment with her hand on it, then
twisted and pushed. The watchers peered intently

77

as the door swung inward, but from where they were they couldn't see anything beyond it except darkness. They watched Ellie-May walk into that darkness and close the door.

'Phew!' Gary moved from the door again, shaking his head. 'I don't get it, Trot. What does she do in there?'

The other boy shrugged. 'I don't know, do I?'

'Does anybody fancy having a look?' whispered Lisa.

Gary looked at her. 'Do you?' She shook her head.

'I think we should wait here till she comes out,' said Fliss.

They waited. Half-past twelve came, and a quarter to one. They didn't take turns now but huddled together, watching the door through eyes that burned, while their feet grew numb. From time to time, faint sounds reached them from beyond the door: sounds which might have made them shiver, even if they had not been cold. It was almost a quarter-past one when the noises ceased, and a few minutes after that when the door opened and Ellie-May reappeared. They watched as she closed the door, crossed the landing and slipped away down the stairs.

'Well,' breathed Gary, 'what now?'

'I vote we go get old Hepworth,' said Trot, 'and

78

let him have a look in that cupboard.'

'No.' Fliss shook her head. 'What if Ellie-May wasn't sleepwalking at all? What if she's been up to something in there – something she shouldn't? We don't know, do we? If we fetch Mr Hepworth we could land her in serious trouble.'

Lisa gazed at her friend. 'Ellie-May's always getting other kids in trouble,' she said. 'I don't think we should worry too much about that.'

Gary nodded. 'I'm with Lisa,' he said.

'Me too,' growled Trot. 'There's something weird going on here, Fliss. We can't keep it to ourselves. Not when Ellie-May might be in danger.'

Fliss nodded. 'OK. I wasn't suggesting we keep it to ourselves indefinitely – just till morning. I'll have a word with Ellie-May before breakfast. Tell her we saw her. Ask her what she was doing. Then, if she doesn't come up with a satisfactory explanation we bring in the teachers. How's that?'

Gary shrugged. 'Sounds fair enough to me. Give her a chance to explain.'

'All right,' said Lisa.

'OK,' sighed Trot. 'I'm too shattered to argue anyway.'

They left the bathroom and tiptoed away to their beds, but dawn was breaking over the sea before any one of them slept.

'Fliss – hey, Fliss!' Somebody was shaking her roughly. She opened her eyes to find Marie grinning down at her. 'Come on, lazybones – you're going to be late for breakfast and it's the abbey today.'

'Mmm.' She pulled up the covers and turned her head away. 'Leave me here,' she mumbled. 'I just want to sleep for ever.'

'You'll write apologies for ever if you make us late. Everybody else has finished in the bathroom and some have gone downstairs.'

Bathroom. Last night. Something she said she'd do. 'Oh, crikey!' She threw back the covers, leapt out of bed and grabbed her towel. 'Listen, Marie – will you do me a favour?'

'What?'

'Make my bed while I get washed? I'm supposed to see Ellie-May. I wanted to catch her before she went downstairs. Please?'

80

'OK.' Marie smiled. 'Just this once. Go on.'

Fliss ran across the landing, forgetting in her haste to check the linen cupboard door. She washed rapidly, splashing a lot of water about. It doesn't seem two minutes since I was in here before, she thought.

When she returned to room ten her bed was neatly made and Marie had gone. She pulled on some clothes, dragged a comb through her hair and headed for the stairs. Five past eight. Breakfast was at eight o'clock. Ellie-May would be in the dining-room by now, with no empty place at her table, and Lisa and the boys would be cursing her for being last again.

The third-floor landing was deserted, which meant that Trot and Gary had gone down. The next floor was Ellie-May's. Fliss ran down the stairs and nearly bumped into Mrs Evans and Mr Hepworth, who were talking in the doorway of room four. She slowed down and tried to creep past, but Mrs Evans said, 'Stop, Felicity Morgan. Come here.'

'Yes, Miss?'

'Yes, Miss? I'll give you "yes, Miss". What time do you call this?'

'Five past eight, Miss.'

'Nearly six minutes past, actually. And what time's breakfast?'

'Eight o'clock, Miss.'

'Exactly. So you're six minutes late. And you were running. Why were you running, Felicity?'

''Cause I'm six minutes late, Miss.'

'Don't be cheeky! You've broken two rules already. Mrs Marriott will be in the dining-room. Tell her Ellie-May's not well, and that Mr Hepworth and I will be down in a minute. Have you got that?'

'Yes, Miss.'

'Off you go then. And think on – I'll be watching you, Felicity.'

She hurried on down. She didn't run, but her mind was racing. Ellie-May's not well and there are two teachers outside her room. She's in bed, then. That means I won't get to talk to her, so what do we do – keep quiet about last night, or tell the teachers? Tell, I suppose.

Everybody was eating cornflakes. Trot gave her a dirty look as she walked in. Mrs Marriott was sitting alone at the teachers' table, chewing watchfully.

Fliss delivered her message, and was sent down to the kitchen to apologize to Mrs Wilkinson for being late, and to ask if she might have some cornflakes. As the woman shook cereal into a bowl for her, Fliss said, 'There's an old lady sits in the shelter across the road.

She seems to be there all the time. Who is she?'

Mrs Wilkinson smiled, pouring milk. 'You must mean old Sal,' she said. 'Sally Haggerlythe. She's mad, I'm afraid. Got some sort of bee in her bonnet about this place – mumbles on about fate and doom and dread and I don't know what. I'd steer clear of old Sal if I were you.'

Fliss said nothing, but thought it might be interesting sometime to have a word with mad Sal Haggerlythe.

She carried her cereal bowl to the dining-room and slipped into the only empty place. None of the other three was at her table, but two tables away sat Gary, facing her. He was looking at her with an expression which was angry and questioning at the same time.

She began mouthing at him, voicelessly, exaggerating her lip-movements and pointing to the ceiling. She's in bed, she mouthed. Sick. I didn't get to talk to her. She spread her hands, palms upward, and shrugged. What do we do?

Gary might have been good at all sorts of things, but lip-reading wasn't one of them. He glared at Fliss, scowling and shaking his head. She began again, even more slowly, stretching her lips and jabbing at the ceiling, then bent forward, goggle-eyed, clutching her throat and shooting out her tongue as if puking into her bowl.

'What on earth's the matter with you, Felicity Morgan?' Mrs Marriott was looking at her as though at a lunatic.

'She's lost her marbles, Miss,' said Gary, and some of the kids sniggered.

'Nobody asked you, Gary Bazzard. Well, Felicity?'

'I had a bit of cornflake stuck in my throat, Miss. It's gone now.'

'I'm glad about that,' said the teacher, acidly, 'because, you see, the rest of us have finished our cornflakes and Mr Wilkinson is waiting to clear, so that Mrs Wilkinson can serve sausages and bacon before they go cold.'

'Yes, Miss.'

She spooned cereal into her mouth and chewed, keeping her head down. Everybody was looking at her. She could feel their eyes. She ate distractedly, thinking about mad Sal and the whispering voice of her dream. It seemed like hours before her bowl was empty.

When everybody had finished breakfast, Mrs Evans stood up and said, 'Now – I want you all to go back to your rooms and get ready for our walk. We're running a bit late, so you haven't got long. I'd like everybody in the lounge, kitted up and ready to go, by nine o'clock. What time did I say, Felicity Morgan?'

'Nine o'clock, Miss.'

'Right. Table one, off you go.'

Felicity's was the last table to be dismissed, but the others were waiting for her outside Gary and Trot's room on the third landing.

'What was that pantomime you were putting on for me down there?' demanded Gary. 'I couldn't make head nor tail of it.' He was holding the giant stick of rock, which he'd sucked almost to a point at one end. He sucked it now as he gazed at Fliss. She shuddered.

'I don't know how you can,' she said, 'straight after breakfast. Mrs Evans and old Hepworth were by Ellie-May's door when I came down, so I didn't get to see her. That's what I was trying to tell you.'

'The point is, what do we do?' said Lisa.

Trot looked at Fliss. 'There's nobody by Ellie-May's door now, is there? The teachers are all downstairs. You could go and talk to her, like you were going to.'

Fliss shook her head. 'The other kids're there. She wouldn't tell me anything in front of them, would she?'

'I reckon we'll just have to tell about last night,' said Gary. 'She was poorly yesterday, and now she's worse. Who knows what might happen if we keep it to ourselves? I think you should go to Mr Hepworth, Fliss.'

'Why me?'

Gary grinned. 'He'd never believe me, nobody does, but he'll believe you. And anyway, the whole thing was your idea, wasn't it – keeping watch and that?'

'All right.' Fliss nodded. 'But I still wish we could have talked to Ellie-May first.'

She found Mr Hepworth in the downstairs hallway, handing out packed lunches. There was a queue. Fliss tagged on the end. When she got to the front she took the little packet he offered and said, 'Sir, can I have a word? It's about Ellie-May.'

'What about Ellie-May?' Kids were waiting in line behind her and he was anxious to give out the rest of the lunches.

'It's about what's wrong with her, Sir.'

'And what's that to do with you, Felicity?'

'Sir, I think I know why she's ill.'

'Indeed? It's Doctor Morgan now, is it? Go on then – why is Ellie-May ill?'

'She goes in the cupboard on the top floor, Sir. At night. I heard her on Monday night, and David Trotter saw her. And last night four of us kept watch and she went in again.'

Mr Hepworth looked at her. 'Are you trying to

86

wind me up, Felicity Morgan? Ellie-May Sunderland's a sensible girl. Why on earth would she be creeping about in the middle of the night, getting into cupboards? I never heard anything so daft in my life.' He smiled thinly. 'Just as a matter of interest, who were the three who kept this watch with you?'

'Lisa Watmough, Sir, And David Trotter and Gary Bazzard.'

'Ah! I thought Gary Bazzard's name might crop up. He put you up to this, didn't he?'

'No, Sir. We saw her, Sir, honestly. There was a thirteen on the door and it's not there in the day-time.'

The teacher's lips twitched. 'And somebody lives in the cupboard, right? Now let me guess who that might be.' He looked at the ceiling for a moment, then slapped his hands together. 'I know – it's Dracula, isn't it?'

Fliss gazed at him, appalled. 'D'you – d'you think it could be, Sir?'

Mr Hepworth looked at her. The smile faded from his eyes. 'Good heavens, Felicity, I do believe you're serious. Somebody's frightened you half to death, haven't they? Now who's been telling you stories, eh? Gary Bazzard, was it?'

'No, Sir. It's not a story, Sir. Honestly. Will you have a look in the cupboard?'

The teacher sighed, gazing at her now with sympathetic eyes. 'All right, Felicity. I'll have a look, and you'd better look too. A cupboard's just a cupboard, as you'll see.' He looked along the line of waiting children. 'Waseem – come and give out the rest of these lunches, will you?'

'Sir.'

Together they climbed to the top of the house and crossed the landing. Fliss hung back as Mr Hepworth twisted the doorknob and pulled. Nothing happened. 'It's locked,' he said.

'You pulled, Sir,' said Fliss. 'Try pushing.'

'There's no point, Felicity – it opens outwards.'

'Ellie-May pushed it last night, Sir.'

'But that's impossible, Felicity. It's made to open outwards – you can tell by the hinges.'

'Get the key, Sir – please.'

He sighed. 'If it's locked now, it must have been locked last night. I think you had a nightmare, Felicity. You dreamed you were watching, but you were asleep. Dreams can seem very real sometimes, but if it'll set your mind at rest I'll go and ask Mrs Wilkinson for the key. Wait here.'

She waited till he turned on the half-landing and passed from sight, then followed quickly, seizing her chance.

The door of room four was closed. Fliss twisted the knob and pushed gently, praying that neither

Mrs Evans nor Mrs Marriott would be in the room.

They weren't. The room, like her own, contained a double bed and a pair of bunks. Ellie-May was in the bottom bunk. She lay on her back with her eyes closed. Her face was almost as white as the pillow. Fliss knelt down and touched her shoulder.

'Ellie-May. Are you awake? It's Fliss.'

Ellie-May's eyelids fluttered. She rolled her head towards Fliss and mumbled, 'What? Oh, it's you. I thought everybody'd gone out. What d'you want?'

'I want you to tell me what happens in that cupboard, Ellie-May. I want you to tell Mr Hepworth too.'

Ellie-May's brow puckered. 'Cupboard?'

'On the top floor. You went there last night. We saw you.'

'No.' She shook her head. 'Nowhere last night. Here. Not very well. Flu, Mrs Evans says. Tablets make me sleepy. Give me dreams.'

'What sort of dreams?' she tightened her grip on the other girl's shoulder. 'What sort of dreams, Ellie-May?'

Ellie-May grimaced. 'Horrible dreams. Dark house. Empty, I think. Stairs. Lots of stairs, and a room. The room of – oh, I forget. Why don't you bog off and leave me alone? I'm off to sleep.'

She rolled her head towards the wall, and the movement exposed the side of her neck. Fliss's eyes widened and she almost cried out. In the pale skin under Ellie-May's ear were two spots of dried blood.

As she stared at the marks on the sick girl's neck, Fliss heard footfalls on the stair. Mr Hepworth was on his way up with the key. She didn't know whether to rush out and drag him in now, or wait till he'd seen inside the cupboard. The cupboard, she decided. Once he'd had a look in there he surely wouldn't need any dragging.

She waited till he'd passed by, then left the room and followed him up. When she reached the top landing he was there, dangling a key on a piece of thick string. He said, 'Where've you been? I told you to wait here.'

'I had to go to the bathroom, Sir. I was scared to use this one.'

He looked at her and shook his head. 'Silly girl. Now watch.'

He inserted the key in the lock, twisted it and pulled. The door opened. Fliss saw darkness and hung back. The teacher beckoned. 'Come along,

Felicity – you're the one who thought we should look inside.' She moved forward and looked.

It was just a cupboard. A walk-in cupboard with a narrow gangway between tiers of shelving. Stacked neatly on the shelves were sheets, pillowcases and towels. Two metres from the threshold, the gangway ended in a blank wall. There was nothing else.

'There you are, you see.' Mr Hepworth closed and re-locked the door. 'No bats, no monsters and no number thirteen. Does that make you feel better?'

Fliss shook her head. 'It's different at night, Sir. It changes. Could you keep the key and look tonight?'

'Certainly not!' He gave her an angry look. 'Now see here, Felicity – this nonsense has gone quite far enough. You asked me to come up here. I was busy, but I came. You asked me to fetch the key. I did. You've seen for yourself that this is just an ordinary cupboard. Either you had a nightmare in which it became something else, or this whole thing has been a silly prank dreamed up by Gary Bazzard. Either way, it stops right here. D'you understand?'

Fliss nodded, looking at the floor. There was an aching lump in her throat and she had to bite her lip to keep from crying. What about Ellie-May?

Those marks. What would he do if she mentioned them now? Go out of his tree, probably. Yet she must tell him. She must.

'Sir?'

'What is it now?' He was striding towards the stairs.

She trotted at his heels. 'Ellie-May's got blood on her neck, Sir. Dried blood.'

They began descending, rapidly. Without looking at her he said, 'Rubbish, Felicity Morgan! Absolute rubbish. One more word out of you, and you'll find yourself writing lines this evening while everybody else goes swimming. Right?'

Right. Miserably, she followed him down. Everybody was out on the pavement, waiting for them, hacking at the flagstones with the toes of their strong boots and scowling into the hallway. All except Ellie-May.

Hallway – Ellie-May – Bed – Dread.

Dead.

They walked through the old town, up the one hundred and ninety-nine steps and across the graveyard to the abbey. They were in their groups, so Fliss didn't get to talk to Lisa who, with Trot, was in Mrs Marriott's group. She talked to Gary, who these days always smelled of peppermint. She told him how she'd seen inside the cupboard, and that it was just a cupboard. She told him how sick Ellie-May looked, and about the blood on her neck. When she told him about the blood, his cheeks went pale and he whispered, 'Crikey – are you sure, Fliss?' She assured him she was, absolutely sure.

He told her he'd overheard Mrs Evans and Mr Hepworth talking. Mrs Wilkinson had been there too. They were discussing Ellie-May. Mrs Evans said she thought they should phone Ellie-May's parents. Mr Hepworth was in favour of waiting another day – it was probably just a touch of flu, he said. Mrs Wilkinson mentioned homesickness and the change of water. It happened all the time, she assured them. Children were in and out of The Crow's Nest every week between Easter and October, and in nearly every group there was one child who grew pale and listless and lost its appetite through homesickness and the change of water.

'I didn't hear the end of it,' said Gary, 'but I think they decided to wait till tomorrow.'

Fliss scowled. 'Grown-ups are so stupid,' she muttered. 'They never believe anything you tell them. If Ellie-May goes in that cupboard again tonight it might be too late to call her parents.'

'What're we going to do? Shall I have a go at talking to old Hepworth?'

'No. I told you – he thinks the whole thing's a tale and that it was you who made it up.'

'Yeah,' sighed Gary. 'He would. I always get the blame for everything. It's the same at home.'

'When we're looking round the abbey,' said Fliss, 'they won't keep us in our groups. Let's talk to Trot and Lisa – see what they think.'

There wasn't much left of the abbey – just some crumbling sections of wall, very high in places, with tidy lawns between. There were a lot of sightseers though, including other school groups, and it was easy for Fliss and the other three to get together behind a chunk of ancient masonry and talk. Fliss told Trot and Lisa her story, and they tossed ideas back and forth. In the end it came to this. None of the teachers would believe them, so they were on their own. They were all agreed that Ellie-May must not be allowed to enter the cupboard again, so they'd watch and if she came they'd stop her, by force if necessary.

'Right,' said Fliss. 'That's settled. Now, d'you think we can forget about Ellie-May and that ghastly cupboard, just for a few hours, and have some fun? We're supposed to be on holiday, you know.'

Gary pulled a wry face. 'It won't be easy, Fliss.'

Trot shrugged. 'I'm scared as a rat thinking about tonight, but what's the point? Fretting isn't going to make it go away, so we might as well enjoy ourselves while we can.'

'Trot's right,' said Lisa. 'We're on holiday. Let's at least explore some of these ruins before the teachers get bored and call us together.'

They split up and wandered about, gazing at the walls and the high, slender windows. Fliss tried to imagine what the place must have looked like long ago, with a roof, and stained glass, and flagstones where all this grass now grew, but it was impossible. Anyway, she told herself, I like it better as it is now. You can see the sky. There are birds, and grass, and sunlight, and I don't like gloomy places.

She shivered.

They stayed an hour among the ruins, then assembled for the clifftop walk to Saltwick Bay. It was just after eleven o'clock. The sun, which had shone brightly as they left The Crow's Nest, was now a fuzzy pink ball. A cool breeze was coming off the sea, and the eastern horizon was hidden by mist.

Mr Hepworth gazed out to sea. 'This mist is known as a sea-fret,' he told them, 'and sea-frets are very common on this coast. You probably feel a bit chilled just now, but once we start walking you'll be all right.' He turned and pointed. 'That collection of buildings is the Coastguard Station. The path goes right past it, and that's where this morning's walk really begins. Who can tell us what coastguards do? Yes, Keith?'

'Guard the coast, Sir.'

'Well, yes. What sort of things do they look out for, d'you think?'

'Shipwrecks, Sir. People drowning and that.'

'That's right. Vessels or persons in trouble at sea – including those silly beggars who keep getting themselves washed out on lilos and old tyres. They also watch for people stuck or injured on cliffs, and for distress rockets and signs of foul weather. Right – let's go.'

They filed across the Abbey Plain and up past the Coastguard Station. The path was part of the Cleveland Way, and countless boots had churned it into sticky mud, permanent except in the longest dry spells. Because of this, duckboards had been laid down, so that most of the path between Whitby and Saltwick was under wooden slats.

'What a weird track,' said Maureen. 'It's like a raft that goes on for ever.'

'I hope it doesn't go on for ever,' her twin retorted. 'It kills your feet.'

It didn't go on for ever. They'd been walking twenty-five minutes, on the flat and over stiles, when the boards ended and they found themselves on a tarmac road which went through the middle of a caravan holiday camp. Just beyond the camp was a muddy pathway which led from the clifftop to the beach. Mr Hepworth lifted his hand.

'Right. This is Saltwick Bay.' He looked at his watch. 'It's twenty-five to twelve, and if it stays fine we'll be here till about half-past four, so there's plenty of time. We'll eat lunch at half-past twelve. In the meantime you may paddle, play on the sand, look for fossils in the cliff-face or collect shells and pebbles on the beach. You are not, repeat not, to do any of the following: sit down in the surf and get your clothing wet. Attempt to climb the cliff. Throw stones or other hard missiles. Murder one another. Chuck your best friend into the sea. Utter shrieks, bellows or similar prehistoric noises, or find a tiny child with a sandcastle and flatten the sandcastle, the tiny child, or both. Is that clear?'

It was.

The bay was sandy in some parts and rocky in others. Fliss and Lisa sat on a rock to remove their boots and socks, then ran down to the water's edge, where they rolled up their jeans and waited for a wavelet to wash over their feet.

'Ooh, it's freezing!' Fliss scampered clear and stood with her hands in her anorak pockets, curling her toes in the wet sand. Lisa gasped and screwed up her face but refused to budge. The wavelet spent itself and rushed back.

'Hey, that's weird!' She flung out her arms for balance. 'If you look down when the wave's going back you seem to be sliding backwards up the beach at terrific speed – like skiing in reverse. I nearly fell over.'

'I remember that from when I was little,' said

Fliss. 'It happened the first time I ever paddled. I howled, and it was ages before my mum could get me in the sea again.'

'There's something else as well,' laughed Lisa, as a second wavelet ran back. 'The water washes the sand away from under your heels. It's like a big hole opening up to swallow you. I bet that's why you were frightened. Come and have a go.'

They played along the edge of the sea till it was half-past twelve and Mrs Evans called them to come and eat lunch. They sat on rocks and munched, burying their feet in the dry sand for warmth.

'I'd no idea it was lunchtime,' said Fliss. 'We only seem to have been here about five minutes.'

'That's 'cause we're having fun,' Lisa replied. 'If it was maths, it'd seem like five hours.'

Grant Cooper and Robert Field had been looking for fossils along the foot of the cliff. They'd dug some out and brought them back in a polythene bag. Mr Hepworth tipped them on a flat rock and spread them out. Everybody gathered round, and the teacher picked out the best specimens.

'Look at this.' He held up a slender, cylindrical object which came to a point at one end. 'This is a belemnite. It lived in the sea millions of years ago and looked something like a squid.'

'It looks something like a bullet now,' observed Andrew Roberts. Mrs Evans gave him one of her looks.

'And this one's a gryphia, or devil's toenail, to give it its popular name. It looks similar to a mussel, but it too lived millions of years ago. And this,' he held up a thick disc with a curled pattern on it, 'is an ammonite. It looks snail-like, and you might think it slithered slowly along the seabed but it didn't. It swam, catching its food with its many tentacles.'

'How do they know, Sir?' asked Haley Denton.

'Know what, Haley?'

'That it swam about, Sir. There were no people then, and there are no ammerites or whatever now, so how do they know what it did?'

'Ah – good question, Haley. Well, one thing they do is look at creatures which are built in a similar way, and are alive today. There's a creature called the nautilus which is something like an ammonite. They know how it gets around, so they're pretty sure the ammonite got around in a similar way. D'you see?'

'Yes, Sir.'

When everything had been eaten and washed down with canned pop, the children went off in twos and threes to do whatever they felt like doing. It was a quarter-past one. The mist had thickened, blotting out the sun, and the breeze gusted spitefully, sharp with blown sand. The holidaymakers had withdrawn to their caravans, so that the children of Bottomtop Middle had the beach to themselves. They went barefoot, but did not remove their anoraks.

Fliss and Lisa ranged far along the tideline, looking for shells and fancy pebbles. They found no shells, except some blue-black fragments of broken mussel which they spurned. There were plenty of pebbles though, and some were quite pretty, especially when wet. They picked up the best ones, putting them in the bags they'd saved from lunch. It was absorbing work, and when Fliss finally looked up she was amazed to see how far they'd come.

'Hey, look – we're miles from anyone else. The teachers look like dots.'

'That's just how I like them,' chuckled Lisa. 'We can't go any further, though – we've run out of beach.'

It was true. In front of them a great, dark headland jutted into the sea. Gulls skimmed screaming along the face of its cliff but the still air felt less cold.

'There's no wind here,' said Fliss. 'Let's stay for a bit. Look – the tide's swept all the rubbish into a corner like Mrs Clarke at school. There might be something good.'

They waded through the flotsam with their heads down, turning it over with their feet, exclaiming from time to time as some new find came to light. A lobster pot smashed in a storm. A clump of orange line, hopelessly tangled. A dead gull.

Fliss worked steadily along the base of the cliff, seeking mermaids and Spanish gold. She heard the hiss of surf on sand, and glanced up to find she'd almost reached the sea. As she stood looking out, her eyes were drawn to a dark, spray-drenched rock, and to the bird which sat on it.

It was black, and it held out its ragged wings as though waiting for the wind to dry them. Fliss shivered as she gazed at it, feeling the magic drain out of the day. It reminded her of something. A witch perhaps, or a broken umbrella. Or the iron crow on the Gate of Fate.

When Fliss and Lisa got back, the teachers had already called everybody together for the return journey. It was only a quarter-past three, but the mist had thickened and there was a hint of drizzle in it. Some of the kids were sitting on rocks, drying their feet with gritty towels, pulling on socks and boots. Others stood waiting with their hoods up and bags of pebbles dangling at their sides. A small party, supervised by Mrs Evans, was picking up the last scraps of litter. Bottomtop Middle prided itself on the fact that whenever a group of its children vacated a site, they left no evidence that they had ever been there.

As they trudged up towards the path in the cliff, Fliss saw a large, slate-coloured pebble lying on the sand. Something about it appealed to her – its perfect oval shape perhaps, or its wonderful smoothness. She bent and picked it up. It was thick, and far heavier than she'd expected, and when she tried to add it to the collection in her polythene bag, it wouldn't fit. She was cramming it in her anorak pocket when Mrs Evans, who was bringing up the rear, said, 'Felicity – you don't really want that, dear. It's far too big. You'll be crippled by the time you've carried it all the way back to Whitby, not to mention the fact that it'll probably tear your pocket. Throw it away.'

Fliss was a quiet girl who never argued with her teachers, and so she surprised herself as well as Mrs Evans when she said, 'I like it, Miss. I want to keep it.'

It was lucky for Fliss that Richard Varley chose that moment to leap on Barry Tune's back. As the two boys fell on to the sand, Mrs Evans called sharply and hurried to separate them, and by the time she had done so the line of children was toiling up the cliff path. She had to put on a spurt to catch up, and the pebble incident was forgotten.

The rest of the walk back was uneventful, except that it started to rain in earnest which made the duckboards slippery. Several children fell, to the delight of the rest, who laughed and cheered their classmates' misfortune.

By twenty to five they were back at The Crow's Nest, drenched and happy. They were sent to their rooms to change and to write up their journals. It was during this interlude that Fliss and Lisa, Trot and Gary met briefly on the fourth-floor landing.

'We all set for tonight?' asked Fliss. She felt tense, and was amazed that for a few hours today she'd actually succeeded in forgetting about all of this.

The others nodded. 'Same time, same place,' said Trot. 'And let's hope nothing happens.'

'Any news of Ellie-May?' asked Lisa.

Gary shrugged. 'I saw Mrs Marriott going into her room as I came up. Maybe they'll call her parents to take her home or something.'

'Oh, I wish they would,' sighed Fliss. 'I'm fed up of feeling scared.'

Trot nodded. 'Me too.'

'We all are,' said Lisa. 'Who wouldn't be?'

After tea, everybody had to rest quietly for an hour in their rooms to let their food settle before Mrs Evans took them swimming. Fliss couldn't rest. There was something she had to do. She looked out of the window. Yes, old Sal was there as usual. Mumbling something about going to the toilet, Fliss left the room, slipped down the stairs and let herself out. It was still raining.

The old woman looked up as the girl reached the shelter. Fliss smiled. 'Hello.'

Sal nodded. 'Evenin'.'

Fliss blushed, looking down at her feet. She didn't know what to say.

'I – I'm staying at The Crow's Nest.'

'Aye, I know.'

'I've seen you lots of times. Through the window.'

The crone nodded. 'Windows is the eyes of a house.'

Fliss smiled. 'Yes. Eyes, watching the sea. Lucky old house.'

'Lucky?' Something rattled in Sal's throat. 'You're wrong, child. It's got the other eye, see. The eye that sleeps by day.'

'Oh, has it?' Fliss smiled, not sure whether she ought to. The eye that sleeps by day. Sounds barmy but then, so does room thirteen. Should she mention room thirteen to Sal? No. There wasn't time. It only needed a teacher to look in room ten and she'd be in more trouble. She looked at the old woman. 'I'd better get back. They'll be wondering –' She let the sentence hang, turned and ran through the rain with her head down.

Nobody had missed her, and when the swimming party set out twenty minutes later old Sal had gone. The rain-lashed streets were practically deserted, and when they got to the pool they found that they had it almost to themselves. They made the most of it, leaping and splashing and whooping in the warm, clear water under Mrs Evans' watchful gaze. A puzzled frown settled for a moment on the teacher's face when she noticed four of the children standing by the steps at the shallow end, taking no part in the revelry. Odd, she mused. Very odd. You'd think they were non-swimmers or something, but they're not. Still, it's up to them, isn't it? Perhaps they're tired from the walk today. Her eyes moved on, and the frown dissolved.

21

Nobody called Ellie-May's parents, or took her home. The word was that she was a little better, and might even be with them on the coach to Robin Hood's Bay the following day.

Fliss wasn't fooled. At ten o'clock she was lying on her back, staring at the wire mesh under Marie's mattress, waiting for half-past eleven. Her hands were folded across her chest, and under them was the pebble from Saltwick Bay. She felt its weight when she breathed, and her fingers caressed its perfect, soothing smoothness.

She was tired. Not from swimming – neither she nor the other three had swum – but from the exertions of the day and a sleepless night before. The swimming must have finished off Marie and the twins, because they were zonked out already. She listened to their breathing and wondered if she could stay awake.

She didn't. Not completely. At least twice she

drifted off and woke with a start, thinking she'd missed the witching hour, but there was to be no such luck. When the town clock chimed for eleven-thirty she was wide awake, and scared.

This time she got to the bathroom first. Trot and Gary came nearly straightaway, but it was nineteen minutes to twelve when the door of room eleven opened and Lisa slipped out.

'Sorry I'm late,' she whispered. 'I fell asleep.'

'It's OK,' Fliss told her. 'I fell asleep too – twice.'

'I was spark-out,' admitted Trot. 'This div had to shake me like a madman to wake me up.' He looked at Gary. 'Didn't you, Gaz?'

Gary nodded. 'You should've got yourself a stick of rock like mine. I sucked that from ten o'clock and didn't nod off once.'

'Dirty pig!' shuddered Lisa. 'I don't know how you can.'

Gary grinned. 'You should see it – it's getting a really good point on it now.'

'Tell you what I do want to see tonight,' said Fliss. 'I want to see how the thirteen gets on that door. I want to be watching when the clock starts striking midnight – see the exact moment the number appears.'

'Yeah.' Trot nodded. 'Good idea. Let's do that.'

'I've brought my torch,' said Lisa. 'We can shine

it on the door – right where the number will be. We'll see really clearly then.'

They waited. Gary, sitting on the rim of the bath, looked at his watch every few seconds. Fliss went to the hand basin, ran a trickle of cold water into her cupped hand and sucked it up, watching herself in the mirror. Trot stood by the window, gazing out. The patterned glass splintered the light from a streetlamp. Lisa leaned on the wall by the door, switching her torch on and off.

After a while Fliss whispered, 'Maybe she won't come.'

'It's only five to,' Gary told her. 'Plenty of time yet.' He hoped Fliss was right.

When his watch told him it was a minute to midnight, Gary got up and went over to the door. The others joined him, jostling quietly till they could all see and Lisa was at the front with her torch. 'Thirteen seconds,' he hissed, and began counting down. At fifteen seconds Lisa switched on and steadied the disc of light on the right spot.

It was not spectacular. As Gary whispered, 'Zero,' they heard the town clock chime, then strike. At about the fourth stroke they noticed a small shapeless mark on the door, and Lisa moved the torch slightly to get it in the centre of her beam. It was like a stain, lighter than the surrounding woodwork. As stroke followed stroke, the stain seemed to shrink and become paler, and then to divide, becoming two whitish blobs whose shapes altered until, by the twelfth stroke, they formed the figures one and three. As the echo died, they heard a door close somewhere below.

'I think she's coming,' warned Fliss. 'Switch the torch off, Lisa.' She did so, plunging the landing into darkness. They withdrew and half closed the door again.

'Did you see that?' breathed Trot. 'It just came out of nowhere. I can't believe it.'

Fliss snorted. 'You've got to believe it, you div – you saw it. The point is, what do we do when Ellie-May gets here?'

'We stop her,' hissed Gary. 'By force if we have to. We agreed.'

'OK, but which of us actually goes out there and grabs her – or do we all go?'

Lisa shook her head. 'We can't all go. It'd scare her to death. It should be a girl, Fliss – you or me. But I think we should try calling her first – from here.'

'Sssh!' Trot pressed a finger to his lips. 'She's here.'

They looked out. Ellie-May was standing on the top step, looking at the door to room thirteen. She hesitated for a moment, then moved forward. Lisa nudged Fliss. 'You, or me?'

'Me.' As Ellie-May drew level with the bathroom, Fliss cupped her mouth with her hands and hissed, 'Ellie-May!'

The girl didn't turn or pause, but continued walking slowly towards the cupboard. Using her full voice this time, Fliss called out, 'Ellie-May – over here!'

It made no difference. The girl was standing before the door now, reaching for the knob. Fliss felt a push in the small of her back and Lisa hissed, 'Go on, for heaven's sake – before she opens that door!'

She left the bathroom and moved across the landing, approaching Ellie-May from the rear. As the girl's hand closed round the knob, Fliss took a gentle grip on her shoulder and said, 'Ellie-May – You don't want to go in there.'

She felt the thin shoulder stiffen under her hand. Ellie-May's head turned, slowly, and Fliss found herself gazing into eyes which were dead as a shark's. The girl's lips twitched. 'Let go of me,' she hissed. 'Leave me alone.'

'Ellie-May!' Fliss swung her round and held her by both shoulders. 'Listen. We're trying to help you. If you go in that room, you'll die!'

Ellie-May snarled, shaking her head. 'Never die. Never. You, not me.' She tore herself from Fliss's grip and turned, scrabbling for the doorknob.

'Gary!' cried Fliss. 'Lisa. Quick – I can't hold her!' There was a scampering of bare feet on carpet and they were with her, the three of them. Hands reached out, snatching fistfuls of Ellie-May's clothing, circling her wrists. She hissed and fought, amazingly strong, freeing one hand to twist the doorknob and push.

The door swung inward. Fliss, one arm crooked round Ellie-May's neck, glanced inside and saw not a cupboard, but the room of her dream. There was the table with the long, pale box upon it and beyond, a small, curtained window. A window which wasn't there in the daytime. The eye that sleeps by day! She dug her heels into the carpet, threw her weight backwards and fell with Ellie-May on top of her.

'Quick, one of you – close that door!' She flung both arms round Ellie-May's waist and held on as the girl bucked and writhed. Lisa dropped to her knees, grabbed Ellie-May's legs and fell forward, pinning them under her. Fliss heard the door slam, and then the boys were there, catching the girl's wildly flailing arms. Ellie-May fought on for a moment but they were too many for her. Fliss felt the thin body go limp, and the girl began to cry. When they let go of her she lay curled on her side with a thumb in her mouth, moaning softly.

They got up and stood, looking down at her. 'What do we do now?' asked Lisa.

As she spoke, they heard voices below and footsteps on the stair. 'It won't be up to us,' said Gary. 'Here comes the cavalry.'

22

'What on earth's going on here?' The landing light came on, and there stood Mrs Evans, unfamiliar in a quilted dressing-gown and no make-up. She saw Ellie-May on the floor and hurried forward, dropping on one knee beside her.

'She was – we were –' Fliss floundered, seeking words which might make their story credible, while the teacher lifted Ellie-May's head on to her lap and checked with hands and eyes for damage. Mrs Marriott appeared in a beige nightie, followed closely by Mr Hepworth in maroon pyjamas. The door of room ten opened and Marie's sleepy face peered out.

'Marie Nero!' snapped Mr Hepworth. 'Get back into bed – now!' The door closed. He looked at Ellie-May, sobbing in Mrs Evans' arms, then at Gary, then at Fliss. 'What's all this about, Felicity Morgan – what's happened to Ellie-May?'

'Sir, she came up again. To go in the cupboard, only it's not a cupboard. Look.' She pointed, and then her heart sank. There was no number on the door. 'There was a number, Sir. We all saw it. Thirteen. And Ellie-May opened it and it opened inwards, and inside –' She stopped. There was disbelief in the teacher's eyes, and the hard glint of anger. She dashed across to the door, twisted the knob and pushed.

It was locked. She pulled, but the door didn't move. She turned, pointing. 'Look at Ellie-May's neck, Sir!'

'Yes, look at it,' said Mrs Evans, grimly. She tilted the girl's head to one side and lifted the hair. Ellie-May's neck was bruised and scratched.

'She was fighting, Miss – fighting to get in the room. We had to stop her, Miss.'

'That's enough!' Mrs Evans glared at Fliss. 'If Ellie-May came up here of her own accord, then she was obviously walking in her sleep. It's quite common among young people, and all you had to do was come down and tell me or one of the other teachers. Instead, it seems to me that you woke her in a sudden, violent way and she panicked, as anybody would. You've been silly and irresponsible, and there's to be no more of it. Go to your beds, and in the morning I'll want to know what you, Gary Bazzard, and you, David Trotter, were

118

doing up here on the girls' landing in the middle of the night.'

Ellie-May was helped to her feet and taken away, supported by Mrs Marriott on one side and Mrs Evans on the other. Gary and Trot followed a grim-faced Mr Hepworth downstairs, and Fliss and Lisa were left gazing at each other, nonplussed.

'What can we do?' whispered Lisa, almost crying. 'Nobody believes us.'

Fliss sighed and shook her head. 'I don't know, Lisa. I'm too tired and fed up and scared to think. We'll talk in the morning.'

She crept into bed, and jumped when Marie's voice came out of the darkness. 'What happened?'

Fliss sighed. 'Nothing, Marie. Nothing much, anyway. I'll tell you tomorrow, OK?'

'Promise?'

'Promise.'

'OK.'

She expected to lie awake till dawn, but she didn't. She had just time to wonder in a muzzy way what she was going to tell Marie, before sleep rolled in like a black tide and bore her away.

Thursday dawned clear and sunny after the rain. Ellie–May appeared at breakfast, smiling wanly and saying she was feeling much better. Fliss watched her across the dining-room and wondered if she remembered anything at all about last night. From the way she was behaving, it seemed she did not.

Practically everybody had heard something of the disturbance – even the boys on the first floor – and the talk over breakfast was mostly about sleepwalking. Fliss had told Marie that Ellie-May had been found on the top landing, sleepwalking, and had reacted badly to being woken up. Trot and Gary, she said, were in trouble because they had done the waking. When Marie asked what the boys were doing on the top landing in the first place, she said they'd seen Ellie-May pass their floor and followed her up. It didn't sound too convincing to Fliss, but it had got around.

Trot and Gary had been interviewed by Mrs Evans before breakfast. When Trot started to tell her what he saw as he reached for the door to pull it closed, she cut him off, saying, 'The door opens outwards, David, and anyway it was locked.' And when Gary said there was a vampire in the hotel, she told him not to be so stupid. 'If I catch you spreading that story among the other children,' she said, 'a letter will go to your parents the minute we get back to school.'

They were lucky in a way though. Mrs Evans decided they'd gone to the top floor because they were worried about Ellie-May. 'There was absolutely no need for you to worry,' she told them, 'but I can see you were trying to be helpful, so we'll say no more about it.'

So, in spite of the midnight rumpus, and against all the odds, the four found themselves back in favour, free to join in the day's activities. It was to be a busy day, and Fliss hoped this might help her to forget the horrors of the night. This morning they were taking the coach six miles to Robin Hood's Bay where, according to Mr Hepworth, there was a good beach and quaint, narrow streets. At twelve o'clock they would return to Whitby for a fish-and-chip lunch on the seafront, before being turned loose to do their shopping in the afternoon.

Robin Hood's Bay was good. The sun shone all morning and they ran along the sand and played hide-and-seek up and down the little streets. By the time they piled back on to the coach, everybody had worked up an appetite and fish and chips sounded just right.

When they arrived back in Whitby, the teachers got the children settled on some benches not far from the jetty, and Mr Hepworth chose a boy and a girl to go with him to the chippy. Fliss knew he wouldn't pick her – not after last night – and he didn't. He chose John Phelan and Vicky Holmes, and the three of them went across the road and tagged on the back of the queue. Fliss watched. The service was fast, but the queue didn't get any shorter because people kept joining it. She smiled to herself, wondering what the people behind would say when old Hepworth ordered fish and chips thirty-four times with salt and vinegar.

It took them ten minutes to get served and come staggering back with armfuls of greasy little packets. Mrs Evans and Mrs Marriott gave out the portions, and everybody sat in the sunshine munching, chatting and throwing scraps to a gang of gulls which appeared out of nowhere, on the scrounge.

Gary looked at Fliss. 'Where are you going first when they turn us loose, Fliss?'

She shrugged. 'I don't know. A gift shop, I suppose – I want to get a pressy for my mum.'

'I'm not,' he told her. 'I'm off round that "Dracula Experience" place we saw the other day.'

Fliss pulled a face. 'Haven't you had enough of that sort of thing in real life? I know I have.'

'No! I know what you mean, but this is different – a bit of fun. And anyway, I might find a clue there to the mystery of room thirteen.'

'Will you heck! Anyway, I'm not going – it's the last place I want to be.'

'You're chicken, that's why.'

'Am I hummer! Chicken of some daft show after what we've seen at The Crow's Nest? You must be joking.'

'Come on then – prove it.'

'No way.'

'Like I said – chicken.'

'Naff off, Gary, you div!'

'Chicken!'

'OK then – I'll come, and I bet you're more chicken than me. You were scared spitless Tuesday night – I could tell.'

He scoffed. 'You were, you mean.'

The argument might have continued for ever if Mrs Evans hadn't called everybody together to speak to them. Fish-and-chip wrappers had been gathered up and deposited in bins, and the place left tidy as always.

'Right. This is it – the moment you've all been waiting for. You are free to go off now with your friends and spend what's left of your pocket-money. You may go into shops or, if you must, into amusement arcades, but you must stay on the seafront, on this side of the bridge. There's to be no crossing into the old town, and nobody is to go wandering off up the streets leading to the West Cliff. Mrs Marriott, Mr Hepworth and I will be keeping our eyes open, and we don't expect to see anybody charging along the pavements, shouting. Remember, there are other people here besides yourselves, and they don't want to be shoved into the roadway or deafened by children yelling. And please – ' her face changed, so that she looked to be in great pain, 'think before you buy. Seaside shops are full of cheap, tinselly rubbish which looks tempting, but falls apart if you breathe on it. There are nice things – good things – you can take home to your parents, but you have to look for them. Off you go, then.'

Fliss felt like slipping away with Lisa to look in shop windows, but Gary wouldn't let her. 'Come on,' he demanded. 'You said you weren't chicken, so let's go. Last one there's a plonker.'

In spite of Gary's taunting, neither Trot nor Lisa came with them. The only ones who agreed to come were Gemma Carlisle, and Grant Cooper, who arrived last but offered to break the face of the first person who called him a plonker. They paid their fifty pences and went in.

The first bit was a sort of shop, with mugs, T-shirts and badges for sale. 'Huh!' snorted Gary, 'I don't call this scary.' He bought a badge with a bat on it, and they moved on into a dark tunnel. 'This is more like it,' said Gemma. As she spoke, there was a blood-curdling scream and something brushed Fliss's cheek. She ducked away with a cry, and Grant and Gary laughed at her. They were wading through some sort of smoke or vapour which swirled low down, hiding their feet. In the tunnel walls were windows through which weird scenes could be seen. In one, a coffin-lid was lifted by a ghastly hand. In another, a woman with bloodstained clothing lay on a bed, while a red-eyed vampire leered at her through her window. While Fliss gazed at this scene, wishing she was somewhere else, a hand came out of the darkness. Shrinking from it, she walked right into another which grabbed at her throat. She recoiled and started walking faster, wanting only to get to the end of the tunnel and out into the sunlight. But now the floor was moving, and she had to walk fast just to stay where she was. It was like her dream. She wanted to go one way, but her feet were taking her another. Sobbing, she broke into a run, and after a moment the moving section was behind her. She looked down, and the floor was glass. Under the glass was soil, and in the soil, half-embedded, lay the half-rotted heads of corpses.

She hurried on, feeling sick, looking straight in front of her, thinking, I shouldn't have come. I should never have let that idiot Gary persuade me. She was sweating. The screams were getting louder, and there was a sudden gust of wind. She didn't know where the others were, and she didn't care. She rushed along, her hair and face brushed by unseen things. Through her eye-corners she glimpsed spiders and graves and the toothy grins of skeletons.

She blundered on, and then at last she saw a door with a sign on it. WAY OUT.

Thank goodness. Oh, thank goodness! She pushed. It swung open. No sunlight. No. Darkness, and a standing corpse whose head fell off as she watched.

She swerved and rushed past with her head down, and here was another corpse, blocking the way. She swerved again, and it stuck out a pale, bony hand. Sudden anger rose in her against this ridiculous place, and her own stupidity in coming here. Teeth bared, she struck at the hand, but it caught her wrist and the corpse whispered, 'Wait – I have to talk to you.'

She screamed, snatching back her hand. The corpse made a small, distressed sound like the mew of a kitten, and in that instant Fliss recognized it. It wasn't a corpse. It was the old woman in the shelter. Mad Sal Haggerlythe.

'What – what d'you want?'

'Here – back here where there's nobody.' The old woman took her wrist again, gently this time, and led her through a gap in the tunnel wall. It was dark and cold and seemed to be a sort of storage space, with planks and trestles and paint cans, and a lot of stuff she couldn't quite make out. There was a musty smell.

'Where's this?' She didn't know why she'd allowed herself to be led here – if she'd resisted there'd have been nothing the old hag could have done about it.

'Behind the tunnel,' Sal whispered, 'in the real world.' She chuckled wheezily. 'Folks walk through tunnels all their lives, y'know. All their lives. Gawping in through lighted windows, thinking what they see's real, but it's not.' She laughed again. 'No, it's not. They're in a tunnel, see. Looking at a show. And all the time, the real

127

world's just inches away through the wall. And now and then, just now and then, somebody finds a hole and goes through and sees what's behind it all, and d'you know what they get called then?'

The old woman paused, and Fliss shook her head.

'Mad, that's what. Barmy. They're the ones who know what really goes on – what it's all made of – and they call 'em mad. Lock 'em away, some of 'em. I 'spect they'll come for me one of these days. D'you know what I'm talking about?'

Fliss shook her head again, in the dark. 'No. Not really. I'm sorry.' She wondered where Gemma was, and Gary, and Grant. Out by now, probably. She wanted to be with them. 'Look – I've got to go. My friends'll wonder where I am.'

'Listen, then. You've seen something, haven't you, at The Crow's Nest – something strange? And there's a sick child?'

'Yes,' Fliss murmured, 'but how did you know?'

'I know, because I lived in that place a long time ago, before the Great War. It was East View then, not The Crow's Nest. I went there when I was ten, as a scullery maid. It was a grand house then. Turnbull, they called the people who had it. Mr and Mrs Turnbull and their little daughter, Margaret. It wasn't an hotel, you understand – it was a house. A private residence. You've seen the abbey, haven't you?'

Fliss nodded. 'Yesterday.' She wished the woman would come to the point and let her go. If there was a point. There might not be. That was probably one of the signs of madness. It occurred to her that Sal might be dangerous, and she wondered if she'd find her way back to the tunnel if she had to run.

'Well,' the old woman went on, 'there was a bit more to it when I was your age. A gateway, with a little house. Children kept well away from that gateway after dark, I can tell you. Grown-ups too, come to that. That's where he was, see?'

'Who?'

'Him that's in The Crow's Nest now.'

'Who's in The Crow's Nest? Who is he?'

'I think you know. Anyway, that's where he was. Old gatehouse. Folks who knew, steered clear. Strangers didn't. Not always. Now and then, someone'd vanish. Drownded, we'd say. Fell over the cliff in the dark. We knew better. Anyway, it come nineteen-fourteen, and the Great War. Near Christmas, a German battleship comes and stands off a mile or two and fires on the Coastguard Station. Some of the shells hit the abbey. One gets the gateway, and demolishes the little house. Doesn't demolish him, though, 'cause

129

there's only one way to do that, and you know what that is. Anyhow, he's lost his place and so there he is, in the middle of the night, seeking another. He's got to find it before first light, and you know why. And out of all the houses in the town, he picks East View, and that's the end of it.'

'End of it – how d'you mean?'

'End of it as a place folks can live in in peace. Listen. Margaret Turnbull – little Meg – the apple of her daddy's eye. She falls sick. All through that winter, paler and paler, thinner and thinner. Calling out in her sleep. Doctors come. Specialists. No improvement. Comes a night in early spring, and there's ever such a bang and a clatter and they find her at the foot of the stair, unconscious. Seven year old. Doctor says she's been walking in her sleep. Anyway, the little mite recovers, though it's touch and go for a while, and the minute she's strong enough Master Turnbull sells up and moves on, and we're all let go. Later, we hear the child perks up like magic as soon as she's away from that house. And after that the place stands empty, and folks steer clear, same as they used to with the gatehouse. Somebody comes along and buys it eventually – a stranger, but he has no luck and moves out. Place has kept changing hands ever since. Soldiers were billeted there in the last war, and one disappeared.

Deserted, says the authorities. Or drownded, we say, but it's neither. And now he's got bairns — a fresh lot practically every week, and he'll be laughing, and it's you've got to stop his laughter, Miss.'

'Me?' Fliss peered at old Sal in the gloom. 'Why me? And anyway, how?'

'Why you?' The old woman poked a bony finger into her middle. 'Because you had the dream, that's why. You know — the Gate of Fate. The Keep of Sleep. The Room of Doom and the Bed of Dread. Remember?'

Fliss nodded, shivering. 'Yes.' Her voice was a croak. 'But how —?'

'How do I know? I told you. I can go through the wall. Leave the tunnel. See what's really what. And as for how, you'll be told. Don't ask me who'll tell you, because I couldn't explain — just like you can't explain any of this to your teachers — but believe me, you'll be told. And if you refuse to do it — if you don't do what has to be done — your little friend is doomed, together with those who went before her and all who'll follow. Doomed to wander the earth, for ever. Do you understand what I'm saying, Felicity?'

'You know my name.'

'Oh, yes. Felicity. It means happiness. Did you know that?'

'No, I didn't.'

'Well, that's what it means. And if you can be very brave tonight, you'll let happiness back into that sad house, and into the hearts of more people than you know. Will you do it, Felicity?'

Fliss hesitated. The old woman's words were whirling around inside her head. Strange words. A madwoman's words. Yes, Sal Haggerlythe was mad all right – no doubt about it – completely out of her tree. And yet she knew so many things. The dream. All that stuff in The Crow's Nest. Her name, and what it meant.

She nodded, biting her lip. 'Yes.'

'Good.' A frail hand fell on her shoulder and squeezed. 'You'll succeed, Felicity. I know you will. Off you go now – your friends are worrying.'

Fliss allowed old Sal to take her hand and steer her back to the hole in the wall. Two people passed by, laughing to show they weren't scared. Sal waited till they'd gone by, then whispered, 'Follow them – they're on their way out.' Fliss felt a gentle push in the small of her back. She followed the laughing pair, and when she looked round a moment later, there was nothing to be seen.

24

'Where the heck have you been? We've been waiting ages.'

Fliss had emerged, blinking against the sudden glare, on a narrow street at the back of the building. Gemma, Grant and Gary, keen to move on to the next thing, gazed reproachfully at her.

'Sorry. I got lost.'

'Lost?' sneered Gemma. 'How could you get lost in a tunnel, for goodness sake. You walk through and that's it.'

'And you were miles in front of us,' put in Grant. 'We expected to find you waiting here when we got out.'

Gary grinned. 'You shot off up that tunnel in a heck of a hurry, Fliss. For someone who's not chicken, I mean.'

'Chicken's got nothing to do with it. It was that moving floor. It was like a dream I had – a nightmare. My feet taking me where I didn't want to go.

And then there was this hole in the wall, and I went through and I was behind the tunnel. It was pitch black, and I kept bumping into stuff – rubbish and that. I thought I'd never find my way out.'

'You're a nut,' said Grant. 'I never saw any hole, and if I had I wouldn't have gone through. Anyway, where we going next – amusements?'

Gary shook his head. 'Not me. I don't like fruit machines. You lose all your money. I'm off to the shops.'

'Me too,' said Fliss. She needed to talk to Gary, away from the other two.

'Well, I'm going with Grant,' said Gemma. 'I won two pounds for ten pence on a machine last year, at Blackpool.'

When Grant and Gemma had gone, Fliss said, 'I've got something to tell you, Gary.'

'What?' They were back on the seafront, heading for the gift shops. Gary was walking fast.

'Slow down a bit and I'll tell you. It's not the flipping Olympics, you know.'

Gary stopped. 'Go on then – what?'

She told him about Sal Haggerlythe, and what the old woman had said. When she'd told him about the promise she'd made, she said, 'Will you help me, Gary? I don't think I'd attempt it by myself.'

Gary pulled a face. 'I guess so. I mean, we've been together all the way along, haven't we? Trot and Lisa too. I just don't know what it is we're supposed to do, Fliss.'

'She said we'd be told.'

'Yeah, but she's barmy, isn't she? If I hadn't seen all that weird stuff with my own eyes, I wouldn't believe a word she said.'

'But you have seen it. Old Sal might be mad, Gary, but she knows all about The Crow's Nest.'

'Hmm. Well, we'll just have to wait and see if we're told, won't we? If we're not, I don't see how we can do anything except keep Ellie-May from going in that cupboard.'

They shopped. Fliss bought a brown photo mounted on a block for her parents. It was by somebody called Sutcliffe, who lived a long time ago and was a famous photographer. It showed two children playing with a toy boat. She'd seen one like it, but bigger, on the wall at The Crow's Nest.

Gary found a leather key-fob with the abbey and the word Whitby embossed on it for his dad, and a little vase encrusted with seashells for his mum.

By the time they'd decided on these purchases, it was half-past two. They were due to meet the teachers back at the bandstand at three, so they made their way in that direction and spent the last twenty minutes in the lifeboat museum. Some of the others were there too, and they compared presents and donated their last few pennies to the lifeboats.

At three, Fliss, Gary and the others left the museum and crossed the road to the bandstand, where the teachers were waiting. Nearly everybody was there. The twins weren't, and neither was Trot. Everybody sat down except Mrs Evans, who stood gazing along the seafront and looking at her watch.

The twins turned up. Mrs Evans frowned at them. 'What time were we to meet?' she asked.

'Three o'clock, Miss,' murmured Joanne.

'And what time is it now, Joanne?'

'Miss, eight minutes past. We were on the donkeys, Miss.'

'Hmmm.'

It was almost a quarter-past three when Trot came trudging up the slipway from the beach. He was carrying a torn plastic kite, and looked fed up.

'And where have you been, David Trotter? Do you know what the time is?'

'Yes, Miss. Sorry, Miss. I was trying to mend my kite.'

Mrs Evans looked at the kite. It was made of clear polythene on a rigid plastic frame. It had a picture of a bat on it, but the polythene was badly torn and hung in tatters from its frame. She sighed. 'What was the last thing I said before we went off to do our shopping, David?'

'I don't know, Miss.'

'No, because you weren't listening. I warned everybody not to spend money on cheap, rubbishy goods, David. How much was that kite?'

'One pound forty, Miss.'

'One pound forty, and look at it. Didn't you notice how thin that polythene was? Didn't you realize that the first good gust of wind would rip it to pieces?'

'No, Miss.'

'No, Miss. Well, it did, didn't it?' She turned to the group. 'You know, I sometimes wonder whether the other teachers and myself aren't just wasting our breath talking to you people. First there was Lisa Watmough, going into a shop before we even got here, buying a trashy flashlight which is probably broken already. Then Gary Bazzard spends I don't know how much on a stick of rock the size of a telegraph pole.' Her eyes found Gary, who looked surprised. 'Oh, yes, Gary – I know all about that rock. It's in your room now, melting, with a beard of bed-fluff on it. You've sucked at it till you're sick of it, and now you don't know what to do with it.' She looked at

Trot again. 'And now you, with your kite. I only hope that next time, if there is a next time, you'll be told.'

You'll be told. Fliss, whose mind had been wandering, looked up sharply. Mrs Evans, talking about –

Buying things. Things you shouldn't. Lisa. Gary. Trot. Why those three? It's a connection, isn't it? Must be. Can't be coincidence, can it? Her heart kicked. You'll be told.

Yeah, but hold on a minute. What about me? I'm one of them. I started it, in fact, and I haven't been in trouble for buying anything. I've been late for breakfast, but that's different. Nobody's said to me, 'You shouldn't have bought that, it's rubbish.' Nobody's –

The pebble. The big pebble. I didn't buy it, of course, but Mrs Evans told me to put it down, and it's a thing, like a torch or a stick of rock or a kite.

That's it. The four of us. Nobody else has been told off for something they've got, have they? She sat, frowning, gnawing her lip.

A torch. A stick of rock. A pebble. A kite.
You'll be told.

They were back at The Crow's Nest by twenty to four, stowing their purchases in their rooms and writing up their journals. It had been their last day, and Fliss wondered why it had had to end so early. It wasn't as if they'd be setting off home at the crack of dawn and needed an early night. They weren't leaving till half-past ten.

Not that an early night would be much use to the four of us anyway, she thought. She had talked briefly to Lisa and Trot on the stairway. They knew what had happened to her today, and had agreed to meet Gary and herself in the usual spot at half-past eleven.

The rest of the kids were feeling a bit down because the holiday was nearly over, but for Fliss, Gary, Lisa and Trot it couldn't end soon enough. They were tired and frightened, and wanted only to be near their parents and to sleep in their own beds.

'Guess what?' said Marie. She was looking out of the window.

'Shut up, Marie,' growled Maureen. 'I'm trying to write.'

'The old witch is there again,' said Marie, ignoring her.

'We know,' said Joanne, impatiently. 'We saw her when we came past the shelter just now. How d'you spell "stake", Fliss?'

Fliss looked up. 'There's two sorts of stake,' she said. 'What're you writing about?'

'A poster I saw in the town. Movie poster. It showed this vampire with a stake through its heart. It said, "Party all night, sleep all day, never grow old, never die, it's fun being a vampire."'

'That sort of stake's S-T-A-K-E,' Fliss told her.

'Thanks.' Joanne bent her head over her work. Marie left the window, sat down at the dressing-table and began to write. Silence reigned.

Fliss chewed her pencil and stared at the carpet. S-T-A-K-E. Stake. A short pole, sharpened at one end, and a mallet to hammer it in with. A flaming torch to illuminate the crypt, and a cross lest the vampire should wake. A stick of rock the size of a telegraph pole, sucked to a point. A pebble too heavy for the pocket. A torch the shape of a dragon. A cross? No cross.

Trot. We've each done our bit, except Trot. Trot must find the cross, then. He hasn't got one that I've ever seen. He didn't buy one today, which was the last chance. He bought –

A kite. That tattered kite on its rigid, cross-shaped frame. That's it!

She was certain, now. You'll be told, Sal Haggerlythe had said, and it was true. Mrs Evans had catalogued the items, and then spoken those very words. You'll be told. The pieces fitted. Every one.

She got up and went to the window. Sal was sitting in the shelter, and seemed to be looking at her. Fliss mouthed a silent 'yes,' and nodded. The woman made no response, but then, the sun was behind the hotel and this side was in shadow.

When they went down to the lounge, the children found out why they'd returned early to the hotel. There was to be a disco for them in the dining-room starting at seven o'clock. They would eat early so that the room could be prepared, and would have plenty of time to wash, do their hair and get into their best outfits before the festivities began.

'It's a farewell disco,' Mr Hepworth told them. 'Farewell to The Crow's Nest, farewell to Whitby. We've kept it a secret till now because we wanted it to be a surprise. It will go on until half-past nine, with a break at eight o'clock for pop, crisps and various other goodies. Mr and Mrs Wilkinson's daughter will be running the disco, and I think it's very kind of them all. Don't you?'

Everybody did. There were three very loud cheers for the Wilkinsons, who came to the doorway of the lounge to hear them, and then it was dinnertime.

As she ate, Fliss watched Ellie-May, two tables away. She'd joined them on the trip to Robin Hood's Bay that morning, and had seemed fine. She'd behaved so normally that at one point Fliss had approached her and spoken, just to see what she'd do. Ellie-May had been her usual rude self, telling Fliss to drop dead, and she seemed normal now too, sitting between Tara and Michelle, boasting about the outfit she was going to wear. She's chuffed to little mint balls, thought Fliss. Looking forward to the disco like everybody else. She doesn't remember a thing about last night. Or the night before. Or the night before that.

Lucky her.

26

'Hey, where's the dining-room gone?' Neil Atkinson, first down in jeans and sneakers, paused in the doorway. Tables and carpet had disappeared. Chairs had been moved back against the walls. Heavy curtains blacked out all the windows. Coloured lights flashed red, then blue, then green, striking sparks from the parquet, leaving corners in shadow. The place looked twice as big as before. At one end, between stacked speakers, a girl stood behind a double-deck. She twitched and writhed as Madonna belted out a number so loud you felt it through your feet.

'Wow!' Sarah-Jane, made-up and dressed to kill, went on tiptoe to peer over the boy's shoulder. 'It's brilliant – like a real disco. What we waiting for?'

They walked out on to the floor, fitting their movements into the beat, beginning to dance. The girl at the deck smiled as her blue face turned to green. Others followed, spilling on to the floor in their finery with grins and exclamations.

It grew hot as record followed record, rising and falling on the twin-deck in unbroken series. The three teachers sat together way back in shadow and watched. Now and then, somebody would go over and try to get them to dance, but they wouldn't. 'My dancing days are over,' they'd say, or, 'I'm waiting for Buddy Holly.' When the break came at eight, everybody was ready for it.

Fliss managed to get the other three in a corner together. Gary had worked up a sweat. His hair was stuck to his forehead. He slurped Coke as she told them what she'd worked out. When she'd finished, he said, 'So what you're saying is, we go in there where he is, and all we've got is a torch, a pebble, a stick of rock and a knackered kite, right?'

Fliss nodded.

'Well, I don't fancy it, I can tell you that.'

'Who does, but have you got a better idea?'

'Sure. We go to bed tonight like everybody else and forget it.'

'And what about Ellie-May? Not to mention all the other kids he's enticed into that cupboard, and all those he will in future if we don't do something about it.'

'It's got nothing to do with us, has it? We've done our best. We tried to tell the teachers but they wouldn't listen. What I mean is, here we are at this disco, right? And everybody's really enjoying it except us. It's been the same all week. Everybody else has been on holiday, but we've been in the middle of a nightmare. Why us, Fliss? Tell me that.'

Fliss shrugged. 'I can't. I don't know why us, Gary, except we've been picked out somehow. You bought that rock and spent three days sucking it to a point. You're part of the team.'

'Big deal.'

She looked him in the eye. 'We can't do it without you, Gary. It needs four. Four things, four people. Are you chickening out?'

He shook his head, looking at the floor. 'I don't suppose so. It's not fair, that's all I'm saying.'

'You'll be there though, at half-eleven?'

'Yes.'

The second half kicked off with the new Bros album. They danced together, the four of them, a little apart from the others. Gary was right, of course. Deep down, each of them felt as he did – that they'd been unfairly singled out. They'd do what had to be done, but their week had been ruined and that was that. They moved mechanically to the music and thought about midnight.

The end came too soon for everybody, except perhaps the teachers, who had sat it all out, waiting in vain for Buddy Holly. At half-past nine the last track faded, the lights came on and the enchantment melted away. Children stood on the scuffed, littered floor, exposed, self-conscious and tired. Mr Hepworth led three cheers and a round of applause for the disc jockey, who grinned, blushed and looked at her feet. After that, they collected jackets, bags and cardigans and went away to bed.

Mrs Evans stuck her head round the door just as Fliss was taking her shoes off. 'Can I see you out here a minute, please, Felicity?'

Fliss sighed, re-tying the laces. 'What's up now, I wonder?'

'You're in bother,' said Marie, cheerfully. She was already in bed. The twins hadn't finished in the bathroom yet.

Fliss went out on to the landing. Mrs Evans had Lisa there too. She spoke quietly to them both.

'Now listen. I know you're both worried about Ellie-May Sunderland, but you needn't worry any more. She's been fine today, but anyway Mrs Marriott and I have decided to take her into our room for the night, just in case she decides to go sleepwalking again. Mr Hepworth is speaking to Gary and David, and we want you

146

all in bed and asleep before the clock strikes ten. Is that clear?'

'Yes, Miss.'

The disco had shattered everybody, and by the time the faraway clock struck ten Marie and the twins were fast asleep. Fliss lay stroking her pebble, wishing she could sleep too. She could have, easily, but she knew if she did she wouldn't wake up till morning.

So. Ellie-May won't be coming. That doesn't mean the room out there won't change though – wish it did. What about the others? Mr Hepworth's spoken to Trot and Gary. They know Ellie-May's being guarded. Will it stop them coming? Gary wasn't too keen to begin with. And if they don't come, what do we do, Lisa and me? Shine the torch in his eyes and hit him with the pebble, or call it off and let him go on luring kids to their doom? And anyway, who says Lisa's going to show up?

Good way to keep awake, worrying like this. Every quarter that clock chimes, but it seems like hours between. Ten fifteen. Ten thirty. Ten forty flipping five. Forty-five minutes to go.

Then what?

They came. All of them. Fliss came last, clutching her pebble.

'Have we all got our stuff?' she whispered. They showed her. 'Right.' She looked at her watch. Twenty to twelve. 'Soon be over now.'

'Aye,' growled Gary. 'One way or the other.'

Fliss looked at him. 'We're going to succeed, right?'

He shrugged. 'If you say so. But if somebody had told me last week I'd be risking my life for Ellie-May Sunderland I'd have told him he was nuts. I don't even like her, for Pete's sake.'

'Who does, but it's not just for Ellie-May, Gary. Old Sal says it's for all the others.'

'Yeah, well, like I said before, she's crackers.'

They waited. Fliss kept looking at her watch. When it said five to twelve she whispered, 'Right. Time to get into position.'

They'd worked it all out beforehand. Trot was first. He opened the bathroom door and stood on the threshold, holding his kite. He'd stripped away the tattered polythene. All that remained was a stiff, white plastic cross. As soon as the number appeared on the cupboard door, he was to cross the landing, open the door quietly and walk in, holding up the cross. That was in case the vampire was awake and out of his coffin. If he was, then they wouldn't be able to carry out their plan, but the cross might keep the creature at bay till they could get out and slam the door.

Behind Trot stood Lisa with the torch. She would follow him in, and shine the torch around to see if the vampire was loose. If he was, she'd try to dazzle him while they retreated. If he was in the coffin, she was to shine it on his chest, right where Gary had to place the stick of rock.

Gary was third. He would follow the other two in, and if everything was all right, he'd grip his rock with both hands and place the point directly over the vampire's heart.

Fliss would be last. If the vampire was out of the coffin, her job would be to get out fast and that was all. If he was in the coffin, she would raise the pebble and bring it down on the rock, driving the point into the vampire. She was to hammer the rock again and again till the vampire was dead.

It would all have to be done very quickly. Fliss wished they'd been able to practise a couple of times, but they hadn't. So. They had to get it right first time, or else –

The town clock began to chime. 'Stand by,' whispered Fliss from the rear. Her mouth was bone-dry. Her left hand was resting on Gary's shoulder and she could feel him trembling. In front of him, Lisa switched on her torch and trained it on the door.

The pale stain appeared. Four pairs of eyes watched it form the number thirteen. As the figures grew clear, Fliss hissed, 'Go!'

Swiftly, silently, they padded in line across the landing. Trot twisted the doorknob, pushed, and walked into the darkness, holding the cross up high and with Lisa at his heels. The torch beam made a quick sweep of the room and steadied on the long, pale box. Gary strode forward and leaned over the open coffin, grasping the rock in both hands. Fliss stood poised, the great pebble raised high above her head. The torch beam slid over the rim of the box.

He lay with his hands crossed on this breast and his eyes closed. He was thin, and small, and dirty. His face was dead white, except for a dark smudge on the forehead and a brown crust about the bluish lips. A fleece of pale, tangled hair, grey with dust, covered the skull, falling on to the bed of earth which covered the bottom of the coffin. His fingernails were split and blackened, and a disgusting smell rose from the single, filthy garment he wore, which looked like a nightshirt or shroud.

'Ugh!' Gary's stomach heaved and he twisted his face aside.

'Quick!' hissed Lisa. 'His eyes are moving – look!'

As she spoke, the vampire's eyelids fluttered. Gary sucked in some air, turned back and planted the spike he'd made in the vee between the creature's hands. The vampire's eyes flew open, red-rimmed, filled with fear. Grabbing the coffin-rim with one hand and scrabbling in the earth with the other, he began to rise. His lips parted. Chipped, yellow fangs glistened in the torchlight and the breath hissed stinking through his teeth. Trot dashed forward and thrust his cross at the contorted face. The vampire let go of the coffin-rim to strike at it, and as he did so Gary threw all this weight forward, bore down on the spike and yelled, 'Now, Fliss – now!'

Fliss aimed, screwed up her eyes and brought the pebble down with all the force she could muster. There was a wet thud and the vampire began to scream, bucking and thrashing so violently that the coffin slid about. Gary fell forward across the table, clinging desperately to the spike. 'Again!' he gasped. 'For Pete's sake hit it again, Fliss!'

Fliss, sickened, raised the pebble and brought it down again, driving the spike clear through the writhing body into the bloody earth beneath, where it broke off. The vampire screamed again, clutching at the coffin-rim with both hands, flailing its naked legs and arching its back so violently that Gary's grip was broken and he crashed to the floor.

At once the others closed in. Lisa's beam lanced into the creature's fear-crazed eyes. Trot lowered the cross till it almost touched the coffin-rim, and Fliss lifted the pebble, ready to split the vampire's skull.

She didn't have to. As they watched the creature's struggles began to subside. Its screams became ghastly, bubbling cries as it twisted this way and that, clutching at the impaling spike, striving to draw it out. Soon, weakening, it ceased to kick.

Its hands lost their grip on the spike and slid down the curve of the heaving chest on the glistening earth. It lay, mouth open, gulping at the air, rolling its head and screwing up its eyes as it strove to avoid the light. Gradually its movements became sluggish and its breathing shallow. Then, quite suddenly it seemed, the breathing stopped.

The head rolled over to one side. All movement ceased.

Fliss lowered her arms, dropped the pebble on the table and turned away. Trot let his cross fall to the floor and stood, gazing into the coffin. Gary had picked himself up and was leaning against the wall with this eyes closed, breathing hard, whispering, 'We did it. Wow, we did it,' over and over. Lisa aimed her torch beam at the floor and very slowly followed the puddle of light towards the open door. As she did so there were footfalls on the stair, and voices, and the landing light triggered the shift, so that three frowsy teachers saw four dishevelled children and a cupboard which was locked.

Some mornings are just perfect. You know what I mean. You've slept like a log, you come wide awake and it's sunshine from the word go. Sunshine and birdsong and your favourite breakfast and everybody being nice to you. It sometimes happens to people on their birthday.

Well, that Friday morning at Whitby was one of those, and it wasn't anybody's birthday. There should have been some gloom about because the holiday was over, but there wasn't. Fliss and the other three should have felt dog-tired and maybe a little bit chastened after their horrific adventure, but they didn't. They'd got a terrific telling-off from old Hepworth, of course, but they didn't mind that. An enormous weight had been lifted from them and they walked on air. Nobody thought, Oh, crikey, school. Everybody thought, Oh great, home! It was that sort of morning.

Fliss was hungry. The aroma of sausages, drifting up from the basement kitchen, made her mouth water. Sausages! Her favourite. The cereal was a favourite, too. She shovelled it into her face, watching the teachers.

They hadn't tried to explain to the teachers. There was no point. Grown-ups don't believe anything you tell them. They have to see with their own eyes, and there was nothing to see. Not now.

After breakfast, the children went upstairs to finish packing and tidy their rooms. The door of the linen cupboard was closed, and there was no number on it. Never will be again, thought Fliss. Not even at midnight. She smiled.

In room ten, everything had been packed away. Marie and the twins stood looking out of the window. 'There's no old witch today,' said Maureen.

'Mad Sal's not a witch,' said Fliss. 'And she's not mad either.'

Room ten looked bare without their bits and pieces. It wasn't their room any more and they weren't sorry to leave it. They carried their luggage downstairs and stacked it in the hallway. The coach wasn't due for another hour, so the teachers took them down to the beach where they ran or skimmed pebbles or stood, saying goodbye to the sea, which sparkled in the sun.

The coach was coming at half-past ten. At

twenty past, Mr Hepworth called them together and led them back up the steep pathway.

It was there. The driver was stowing the last of the luggage in the boot. Mr Wilkinson was helping him. Both men whistled as they worked.

The children crossed the road and climbed on board. Fliss and Lisa got seats together. The driver slipped into his seat, grinned at the children through his mirror and told them to hold tight. The engine roared into life. The coach rolled forward. The Wilkinsons stood on the top step, waving. The children waved back. The coach gathered speed. The Crow's Nest fell away behind. They were going home.

Fliss settled back in the comfy seat and sighed. 'It's been a funny sort of holiday,' she said.

Lisa nodded. 'You can say that again. I'm glad we did it, though. We made things better, didn't we, Fliss – I could sort of feel it this morning.'

'Oh, so could I. Everybody could, I think. Mr Wilkinson, whistling. And the driver. Drivers are usually a bit narky when they've got a coachload of kids, but this one isn't. Look at him, grinning in the mirror.'

The coach swooped down into Sleights, then toiled up the road to the moors. Halfway up, Fliss slapped her knee and cried, 'Drat!'

Lisa looked at her. 'What's up?'

156

'I've just remembered – that picture I got for my mum. I put it on top of the wardrobe and I've left it there.'

'Oh, Fliss! Why did you put it there, and not in your case?'

'I had other things to think about, didn't I? Vampires, for instance. I just shoved it any old where and forgot about it.'

'Maybe Mrs Wilkinson'll find it – send it on.'

'How can she? She won't know it's mine. It might have been there weeks for all she knows.' She sighed. 'Poor Mum – no pressy.'

They were on the moors now. Sun and sky, wind and heather. Mr Hepworth stood up. 'If you look back now,' he said, 'you'll get a glimpse of the abbey.'

Everybody stood or knelt, looking back. There it was, a black, dramatic silhouette against the shining sea. As Fliss gazed at it, somebody touched her elbow. She turned, and saw Ellie-May with a little flat package in her hand. 'I heard what you said,' she whispered, 'about your mum's picture. I want you to have this.'

'What is it, Ellie-May?'

'A picture. A Sutcliffe, like the one you lost. I saw you with it yesterday.'

'Well, don't you want it? Didn't you buy it for someone?'

'I bought it for me, Fliss. It was a present from me to myself.' She smiled. 'I bring myself presents all the time. Or rather, I did. I was my favourite person, you see. Now you are – you and Lisa and Gary and Trot – because I know what you did. Here – take it.'

Fliss took the package. She smiled at Ellie-May. 'Thanks.'

'Thank you, Fliss.' Nobody had seen her give Fliss the picture. Everybody was busy looking at the abbey. She slipped back to her seat.

Fliss looked along the coach at Ellie-May, then down at the little package. She smiled.

'So long, Dracula,' she whispered. 'Hi, felicity.'

THE END

ABOUT THE AUTHOR

Robert Swindells left school at fifteen and worked as a copyholder on a local newspaper. At seventeen he joined the RAF for three years, two of which he served in Germany. He then worked as a clerk, an engineer and a printer before training and working as a teacher. He is now a full-time writer and lives on the Yorkshire moors.

He has written many books for young readers. *Room 13* won the 1990 Children's Book Award. *Abomination* won the 1999 Stockport Children's Book Award and was shortlisted for the Whitbread Prize, the Sheffield Children's Book Award, the Lancashire Children's Book Award *and* the 1999 Children's Book Award. His books for older readers include *Stone Cold*, which won the 1994 Carnegie Medal, as well as the award-winning *Brother in the Land*. As well as writing, Robert Swindells enjoys keeping fit, travelling and reading.

ABOMINATION

Robert Swindells

Martha is twelve, and very different from other kids.
No TV. No computer. No cool clothes.
Especially, no *friends*.

It's all because of her parents. Strict members of a
religious group, their rules dominate Martha's life.
But one rule is the most important of all: Martha
must never *ever* invite anyone home. If she does,
their terrible secret - Abomination -
could be revealed...

'A taut and thrilling novel from a master
of the unpredictable'
Daily Telegraph

**WINNER OF THE 1999 STOCKPORT
CHILDREN'S BOOK AWARD**

**WINNER OF THE 1999 SHEFFIELD
CHILDREN'S BOOK AWARD**

**SHORTLISTED FOR THE WHITBREAD PRIZE,
THE LANCASHIRE**

**CHILDREN'S BOOK AWARD *and*
THE 1999 CHILDREN'S BOOK AWARD**

ISBN 0 440 86362 7

THE THOUSAND EYES OF NIGHT

Robert Swindells

The skeleton lay on its back. The jaws gaped and one arm lay across the chest as though flung there to ward off a blow...

The Tangle is a long, narrow stretch of derelict land, a wilderness of weeds and rubbish with an old railway tunnel yawning blackly at one end. No-one – not even bullying Gary Deacon – dares venture farinto its sooty darkness. But it is here that twelve-year-old Tan and his friends make a grisly discovery – a discovery that is plunge them into a terrifying adventure as the tunnel slowly unfolds its sinister secret...

'A tremendous climax'
Growing Point

ISBN 0 440 86316 3

HYDRA

Robert Swindells

*The floater moved out into the barn.
Eyeless, it felt the faint pull of starlight
and followed, passing through the great
open doorway and drifting away
in the dark...*

Friends Ben and Midge are determined to
investigate when mysterious corn circles begin
to appear in the fields around Cansfield Farm.
But when they sneak out at night to explore,
they discover that the corn circles are not the only
mystery at the farm; a dilapidated barn conceals a
terrifying secret. As Midge and Ben uncover the true
horror that is being spawned there, they know that
they must tell someone, warn them of the danger.
But who will believe their incredible story?

'Spine-chilling suspense'
Junior Education

'Compelling'
The School Librarian

A FEDERATION OF CHILDREN'S BOOK GROUPS
PICK OF THE YEAR

ISBN 0 440 86313 9

INVISIBLE!

Robert Swindells

What would *you* do if you could become invisible?

Creep around, unseen? Listen in to other people's conversations? Twins Carrie and Conrad, and their friends Peter and Charlotte do all these things, and much more, when a new girl at school - Rosie - shows them her secret: how to make yourself invisible.

It's exciting, and it's fun. It can also be frightening... and dangerous. Especially when Rosie's dad becomes a suspect in a local crime and the gang go invisible to find the *real* crooks...

A gripping adventure from a master of suspense, author of the award-winning *Room 13* and many other titles.

'Robert Swindells writes the kinds of books that are so scary you're afraid to turn the page'
Young Telegraph

ISBN 0 440 86363 5

TIMESNATCH

Robert Swindells

A miracle time machine – or a horror which could destroy them all?

Ten-year-old Kizzy Rye and her brother Fraser are the only witnesses when the time machine invented by their physicist mother works for the very first time. It travels back to the past, snatches an extinct butterfly and brings it forward in time to the present - alive.

An amazing scientific breakthrough with a horrifying potential. For as the news breaks, Kizzy and Fraser find themselves caught in a terrifying spiral of events, as unthinkable requests threaten to turn their mother's dream into a nightmare. Then a sinister organization apears with a monstrous demand - a demand they are prepared to back up with violence...

'Spellbinding... a stirring achievement, certain to absorb and provoke a wide audience'
The Times Educational Supplement

WINNER OF THE JUNIOR CATEGORY OF
THE 1995 EARTHWORM AWARD

ISBN 0 440 86322 8

BLITZED

Robert Swindells

*Imagine being alive before your parents
were even born!*

George is fascinated by World War Two - bombers,
Nazis, doodlebugs. Even evacuation and rationing
has got to be more exciting than living in dreary old
Witchfield! He is looking forward to his school trip
to Eden Camp, a World War Two museum. But he
doesn't realize quite how authentic this visit to
wartime Britain will be...

A hand reaching out of the fake rubble, a slip in
time, and George has to survive something much
worse than boredom. The rubble is now *real* – he has
slipped through time into 1940s London!

A thrilling drama from a master of suspense,
Robert Swindells.

'A first-rate time-travel story ... Swindells is a
powerful, thrilling writer ... as good as Robert
Westall's classic, *The Machine Gunners*.'
Independent on Sunday

'Entertaining and thought-provoking ...
has a wonderfully satisfying ending'
The Bookseller

ISBN 0 440 86397 X